SCIENTIFIC AMERICAN EXPLORES BIG IDEAS

The Science of Monsters

The Editors of Scientific American

SCIENTIFIC AMERICAN EDUCATIONAL PUBLISHING
New York

Published in 2023 by Scientific American Educational Publishing
in association with **The Rosen Publishing Group**
29 East 21st Street, New York, NY 10010

Contains material from Scientific American®, a division of Springer Nature America, Inc.,
reprinted with permission, as well as original material from The Rosen Publishing Group®.

First Edition

Scientific American
Lisa Pallatroni: Project Editor

Rosen Publishing
Joseph Kampff: Compiling Editor
Michael Moy: Senior Graphic Designer

Cataloging-in-Publication Data
Names: Scientific American, inc.
Title: The science of monsters / edited by the Editors of Scientific American.
Description: New York : Scientific American Educational Publishing, 2023. |
Series: Scientific American explores big ideas | Includes glossary and index.
Identifiers: ISBN 9781684169245 (pbk.) | ISBN 9781684169252
(library bound) | ISBN 9781684169269 (ebook)
Subjects: LCSH: Monsters–Juvenile literature. | Science–Miscellanea–Juvenile literature.
Classification: LCC GR825.S354 2023 | DDC 001.944–dc23

Manufactured in the United States of America
Websites listed were live at the time of publication.

Cover: Kiselev Andrey Valerevich/Shutterstock.com

CPSIA Compliance Information: Batch # SACS23. For Further Information contact
Rosen Publishing, New York, New York at 1-800-237-9932.

CONTENTS

INTRODUCTION

"Monsters aren't real. Now go back to bed."

You probably heard this from your mom or dad when you were younger, afraid of what lurked in the darkness of your room at bedtime. Or maybe you weren't scared of monsters at all but were instead fascinated by them. Maybe you still are.

The monster that lived under your bed probably wasn't real. But to deny the reality of monsters is to deny reality itself. Monsters may not be under your bed, but they are everywhere else.

Rather than dismissing the reality of monsters, this book presents articles collected from *Scientific American* that take monsters seriously and examine them scientifically. Section 1, "Here Be Monsters," introduces multiple concepts of monsters–including Bigfoot, ghosts, and zombies–and explains where they come from and why scientists study them. Section 2, "The Making of a Monster," engages with our abiding fascination with monsters and the ways our interest in monsters can lead to scientific insights, including a genetic study of Bigfoot that enhanced our knowledge of bears. Section 3, "Inside the Minds of Monsters," looks at monsters through the lenses of psychology, neuroscience, and microbiology, comparing what we know about the human mind, the nervous system, and biology with ideas we have about the behaviors and abilities of monsters. This section will help you prepare for the zombie apocalypse. Section 4, "Monsters in Nature," examines the existence of monstrous traits and behaviors in the natural world, including vampire bats, zombie cicadas, and parasites that control your brain.

The monsters discussed in this book are not the monsters of Friday night horror films or Saturday morning cartoons. They are the real-life monsters of vampire bats, mummies, zombie fungus, insects, and parasites. They're the monsters that live in our world as well as our imaginations, that are the objects of science as well as inspiration.

Section 1: Here Be Monsters

The Zombies in Our Midst

By Melanie Tannenbaum

Every Halloween, we find ourselves surrounded by zombies, vampires, ghouls, and other mythical monsters. But even though this is the one day each year that we *consciously* realize we are surrounded by these creatures (at least in their human-costumed forms), are we surrounded by more common forms of these monsters every day without even realizing it?

According to lore, *zombies* are corpses that have been reanimated, either through witchcraft, supernatural forces, or a biological virus, to become an "undead," walking creature determined to feast on human flesh. A zombie apocalypse, therefore, is the mass takeover that would occur when zombies start to overrun the earth, chomping down and taking new victims *en masse*.

When it comes to zombies, it's often difficult to know how to think about them. Are they still (in some way) human, or are they simply mindless, flesh-eating automatons? If your friend, relative, or spouse became "turned" into a zombie, would you still see him or her as the person that you once loved? Or would you recognize that this was a new creature, not the caring person that you once knew?

In everyday life, the process of deciding whether or not to ascribe human qualities like thinking, feeling, and intentional action to people, animals, or objects can be called *anthropomorphism*, or *mind perception*. Though it seems easy enough to determine which objects can think and feel and which cannot, it can be a surprisingly variable endeavor. When people engage in anthropomorphism, they often perceive minds in things that should not really have human "mind" capacities, like animals, nature, or technological gadgets (think about that "evil" photocopier that never seems to work when you want to use it). On the other hand, when people do the opposite and *downplay* the minds of human others, they are engaging in *dehumanization*.

Several things can make people *more* likely to anthropomorphize others and perceive minds where they may not exist. First of all, people might be more likely to over-perceive "human minds" in non-human sources when the sources themselves are behaving unpredictably, especially when the perceivers are distracted or too busy to think hard about the causal chain of events. If you're faced with an unpredictable computer, for example, you might be more likely to spontaneously think of it as "annoying" or "mean," even if you consciously understand that the computer is not intentionally trying to mess with you (one would hope). People might also over-perceive minds when they feel powerless, lonely, or have a chronic "need to belong." For example, people who want to socially connect to others, either for intimacy or for valuable resources to regain power/control, can be chronically motivated to see minds in atypical sources like computers, pets, nature, or the supernatural.

Perceiving minds (and therefore the capacity for behavioral intentionality) can help us satisfy the inherent motivation to "make sense" of a senseless, unpredictable world. In one study, Adam Waytz and colleagues had participants interact with a robot (which they knew was a robot) by asking it ten yes-or-no questions. Unbeknownst to the participants, the robot was generating random answers, either predictably (it answered "yes" 80% of the time) or unpredictably (it answered "yes" and "no" equally often). When participants interacted with the unpredictable robot, they were more likely to attribute human-like, anthropomorphic qualities to the robot, saying that it was more thinking, desiring, intentional, and emotional than the predictable robot, even though participants knew that both of the responders were robots and that they were generating random answers. Furthermore, when participants in a follow-up study were exposed to a separate robot, the ones with the goal to predict the robot's actions were more likely to anthropomorphize the robot by seeing it as emotional, intentional, and capable of human-like thought.

This tells us a couple of things. First of all, in the event of an actual zombie apocalypse, we might be in a fair bit of trouble. If you think now that it would be difficult to axe someone you once loved in the brain before they eat you alive, think about how much more difficult it would be if you were living in an unpredictable environment (as a post-apocalyptic world, almost by definition, must be) and therefore even more likely to ascribe human-like, thinking, feeling capacities to your now-undead friends and relatives.

Second of all, the *reversal* of this phenomenon points to the dismal ways in which we might actually "zombify" the people around us. Just as anthropomorphism occurs when people ascribe human-like, thinking/feeling qualities to the non-human entities around us, dehumanization is the process by which we do the opposite and "represent human agents as nonhuman objects or animals... hence denying them human-essential capacities such as thought and emotion" (Waytz et al., 2010). Just as people who are lonely might be more likely to anthropomorphize, in a frightening inverse of this phenomenon, those who are socially well-connected might actually be less likely to perceive human minds in others, therefore dehumanizing and objectifying them. If someone feels well-connected, they might have a lower amount of motivation to seek out social connections, so they might be more likely to dehumanize others, particularly outgroup members. In fact, people are particularly likely to dehumanize certain types of outgroups—in particular, drug addicts and homeless people are frequent "dehumanization" targets. Finally, just as feeling powerless or like one is living in an unpredictable world can increase anthropomorphism, feeling powerful or like one is living in a stable, predictable world can increase dehumanization as well.

With this in mind, it becomes easy to see the everyday zombies in our midst. In an actual zombie apocalypse, it would likely be even harder than we now think it would be to axe our infected friends and family members, as the loneliness, unpredictability, and general sense of powerlessness inherent in our apocalyptic worlds would make us even more likely to see our once-living, now-zombified kin as thinking, feeling humans instead of rabid, undead monsters. However, we may not have to wait for an apocalypse to understand what it feels like to see the people around us as semi-zombies. If we currently feel powerful, socially connected, or like we are living in a predictable world, we may already be more likely to dehumanize (or "zombify") the people around us...especially if they are members of an outgroup.

Pretty spooky stuff!

About the Author

Melanie Tannenbaum is a freelance writer and science communications consultant currently living in the Bay Area. She received her Ph.D. in social psychology from the University of Illinois at Urbana-Champaign in 2015, where her research focused on the science of persuasion and motivation regarding political, environmental, and health-related behavior.

Born to the Purple: The Story of Porphyria

By Nick Lane

Porphyria is named from the ancient Greek word *porphura*, meaning purple. The Greeks borrowed the term from the Phoenicians, who extracted a purple pigment from purpura mollusks to dye the garments of their royal family. Later, in the Byzantine Empire, the term *porphyrogenitos*, or "born to the purple," literally meant that the imperial heir was born after the father's accession to the throne, in a palace room draped in the color.

However, those with the misfortune to be born to the purple involved in porphyria–a group of diseases that result from abnormal accumulations of red and purple pigments produced by the body, called porphyrins–receive far less than royal treatment. There are at least eight types of porphyria, which vary substantially in their symptoms and severity. Historical victims of the worst, most disfiguring forms may have inspired tales of werewolves and vampires. Even today, managing the disease can be challenging.

Light-Activated Toxins

Hippocrates is often cited as the first to recognize porphyria (which was then referred to as blood/liver disease) but the causal role of porphyrin pigments was only established in 1871 by the great German pioneer of biochemistry Felix Hoppe-Seyer. In 1889, Dr. B.J. Stokvis described the clinical syndrome as "porphyria," and from then on more and more forms of the syndrome were discovered.

All the versions of porphyria have one thing in common: they each result from faults in the body's heme-building machinery. Heme, a component of the oxygen transporter hemoglobin, is made in a sequence of eight steps, as in a factory assembly line. Each step is catalyzed by a separate enzyme. If any of these eight steps fails because of an inherited genetic mutation or an environmental toxin, then the whole assembly line gets jammed. The products of the earlier steps, porphyrin intermediates, may build up to toxic levels. These porphyrins accumulate in the skin and other organs before being excreted in feces and urine (which may turn a port-wine color). Exposed to light, the porphyrins can turn caustic and destroy surrounding tissue.

(Put to medical use, drugs containing porphyrins can attack tumors and other ailments. Unlike most natural porphyrins [but like chlorophyll] these drugs are not purple but green, as they have been modified chemically so that they absorb light at wavelengths that can penetrate into biological tissues. See "New Light on Medicine," by Nick Lane; *Scientific American*, January 2003.)

Exactly which porphyrins accumulate depends on the site of the jam, and it is this that gives porphyria such a wide range of symptoms. The severity of the jam also varies. In some cases the jam is total, preventing any heme synthesis at all. In others, it is only partial, permitting limited heme synthesis. The blockage of the assembly line also means that the body cannot make enough heme to produce normal red blood cells. Some of these abnormal red cells rupture, leading to hemolytic anemia, while the spleen detects abnormalities in other red cells and breaks them down, making matters worse.

Werewolves and Vampires

One of the more common types of the disease is acute intermittent porphyria (AIP), which famously afflicted the unfortunate King George III of Britain–the "mad king" of Alan Bennett's play. In AIP the most notable symptoms are neurological attacks, such as trances, seizures, and hallucinations, which often persist over days or even weeks. Luckily, most people with AIP have a latent form, and never develop any symptoms.

Another relatively common form is porphyria cutanea tardea, which presents a very different spectrum of symptoms. In this case, the hallmark is photosensitivity (an excessive reaction to light), which causes chronic blistering and even burns on sun-exposed areas. Healing is slow and is associated with scarring and hair growth, especially on the face. Most of the time the facial hairs are fine, so the hirsutism is barely noticeable. Sometimes, however, the hair growth can give the appearance of a werewolf, leading to speculations that the myths may have had a medical basis.

In congenital erythropoietic porphyria (CEP), one of the rarest forms, 18 different mutations in the gene encoding the enzyme uroporphyrinogen III cosynthase have been reported in different families. These mutations obstruct heme synthesis to varying degrees, giving a spectrum of severity. At its worst, CEP causes appalling photomutilations from the light-activated porphyrins, including loss of facial features and fingers, scarring of the cornea, and blindness. The condition may have been less rare in the past, especially in isolated pockets where inbreeding could occur, such as the valleys of Transylvania—perhaps giving rise to tales of vampires.

While the accumulation of porphyrins is usually caused by a genetic mutation, toxins (such as alcohol excess) and environmental contaminants can also cause the disease. The most notorious environmental episode happened in Turkey in the 1950s, when 4,000 people developed a form of porphyria after eating wheat seeds that had been sprayed with a fungicide, hexachlorobenzene. Hundreds died, and use of the fungicide was later banned around the world.

Methods of Treatment

In most cases of porphyria, blood or heme transfusions can supply some relief from the symptoms, and this is still the mainstay of treatment. Interestingly, the heme pigment is robust enough to survive digestion, and is absorbed from the intestine (even though the protein parts of hemoglobin are broken down). This means that, in principle, it is possible to relieve the symptoms of porphyria by drinking blood—another possible link with the vampire stories.

Heme infusions help in the treatment of porphyria patients in two ways. First, they overcome the body's shortage of heme, relieving anemia. Second, the extra heme suppresses further heme synthesis via a negative feedback loop. This effectively switches off the assembly line, bringing an end to the production of toxic porphyrin intermediates. Drawing blood (phlebotomy) can also help, because this quickly removes porphyrin intermediates from the circulation. In most cases, some degree of normality can be restored within a few days of an attack.

In the more serious forms of porphyria such as CEP, however, treatments are less effective. Sometimes the spleen must be removed in an attempt to treat the hemolytic anemia. In CEP, the genetic fault affects the stem cells in the bone marrow, which divide to produce new red blood cells. In principle, CEP can be cured by bone-marrow transplantation, which replaces the faulty stem cells with fully functional ones. Bone-marrow transplants have been carried out successfully in at least five children with CEP, usually within the first few years of life. The treatment apparently cures the disease over a period of years.

Future Therapies

But bone-marrow transplantation presents its own challenges, and is considered a last resort. In the longer term, hope to cure porphyria is invested in gene therapy, in which the faulty genes are replaced with functional ones using a virus as a vector (delivery method). The technique has been shown to be effective in cell culture, but there is still a long way to go before gene therapy for CEP can be used in clinical practice.

Other future treatments for porphyria will depend on the results obtained from research with experimental animal–and even plant–models. Some of these are improbable, to say the least. For example, all fox squirrels (*Sciurus niger*) have a gene defect that gives them a form of CEP, yet they do not suffer any adverse consequences, for unknown reasons. Studies of the animals could yield clues that would be useful in fighting CEP.

Surprisingly, even plants–which use the green porphyrin, chlorophyll, to absorb light energy–can suffer from a condition analogous to porphyria. Plants make chlorophyll via a pathway very similar to that for heme production in animals. Mutations in the gene for the final step in this pathway lead to a buildup of porphyrins in the leaves. On exposure to sunlight the leaves blister, and eventually wither and die. The process is so similar to human porphyria that some researchers hope to find a cure for the human condition by studying the properties of so-called "vampire plants," like maize.

About the Author

Nick Lane studied biochemistry at Imperial College, University of London. His doctoral research, at the Royal Free Hospital, was on oxygen free radicals and metabolic function in organ transplants. Lane is an honorary senior research fellow at University College London and strategic director at Adelphi Medi Cine, a medical multimedia company based in London. He is also the author of Oxygen: The Molecule That Made the World, *published by Oxford University Press (2003).*

Mummy DNA Reveals Birth of Ancient Scourge

By David Biello

Centuries of silence cannot keep ancient Egyptian mummies from sharing their secrets with scientists. From archaeologists determining cultural practices to chemists studying embalming, mummies have revealed libraries of information. Now such mummies are also yielding evidence about the diseases of the past by giving up the facts encoded in their preserved DNA, and new research may have pinned down the ancient homeland of a modern scourge.

Leishmaniasis–a disease caused by microscopic parasites, like malaria, and transmitted by sand flies–results in painful skin sores and in its most vicious form causes at least 500,000 deaths worldwide every year. Endemic to northeastern Africa, it also afflicts South and Central America as well as the Middle East; as many as 650 U.S. soldiers experienced it during the first year of the invasion of Iraq. The lethal form–visceral leishmaniasis, also known as *kala azar*, or black fever in the Hindi language of India, where the disease was first discovered by British doctors–is particularly prevalent in Sudan, and some authorities have claimed it originated there.

Albert Zink of Ludwig Maximilian University in Munich and his colleagues tested the DNA of bone samples from 91 ancient Egyptian mummies and 70 from old Nubia–modern Sudan–to determine if they had suffered from leishmaniasis. In nine of the 70 Nubian mummies–taken from graves stretching as far back as A.D. 550–mitochondrial DNA of the parasite was discovered, proving the disease was endemic at least that far back. It likely has even more ancient roots; four of the Egyptian mummies carried the parasite's DNA, each dating from the Middle Kingdom period of 2050 to 1650 B.C. when trade ties with Nubia were strongest. Egyptian mummies from prior and later periods showed no sign of the disease, according to the research in the October issue of *Emerging*

Infectious Diseases. "In this study, we haven't found evidence for *Leishmania* DNA in the samples from the New Kingdom to the Late Period, which are 500 to 1,000 years younger than those from the Middle Kingdom," Zink notes. "Therefore, we think that the presence of leishmaniasis is more due to the close cultural contacts of the Egyptians and the Nubians."

In addition to highlighting the old cultural ties between Egypt and Nubia, it also adds further weight to the theory that visceral leishmaniasis first developed in the region now known as Sudan. And the technique has been applied to other diseases, such as tuberculosis and malaria, to trace their development. "We can contribute to a better understanding of pathogen evolution and, thereby, to a more efficient treatment and control of infectious diseases," Zink says. The pathogens that proved a curse to ancient mummies may yet provide a cure for ancient scourges that still plague humanity.

About the Author

David Biello is a contributing editor at Scientific American.

In a First, Physicists Glimpse a Quantum Ghost

By Karmela Padavic-Callaghan

The wave function—an abstract concept used to predict the behavior of quantum particles—is the bedrock on which physicists have built their understanding of quantum mechanics. But this bedrock itself is not something physicists have a perfect grasp of, literally or philosophically. A wave function is not something one can hold in their hand or put under a microscope. And confusingly, some of its properties simply seem not to be real. In fact, mathematicians would openly label them as imaginary: so-called imaginary numbers—which arise from seemingly nonsensical feats such as taking the square roots of negative integers—are an important ingredient of a wave function's well-proved power to forecast the results of real-world experiments. In short, if a wave function can be said to "exist" at all, it does so at the hazy crossroads between metaphysical mathematics and physical reality.

Now researchers at the University of California, Santa Barbara, and their colleagues have made big strides in bridging these two realms: for the first time, they reconstructed a wave function from a measurement of how a semiconductor material responds to an ultrafast pulse of light. Appearing in *Nature* in November, the team's work may help take electronics engineering and quantum materials design into a new era of fine-tuned understanding and precisely controlled innovation.

For real-world applications, such as modern electronics, the somewhat mysterious wave function is physicists' best source of information about what actually happens inside of some new gadget. To predict how fast an electron moves inside a material or how much energy it can carry, they must start their calculations with the so-called Bloch wave function—named for physicist Felix Bloch, who devised it in 1929. This is especially important for engineering quantum devices, says Joe Costello, a physics student at U.C.S.B. and co-lead author of the recent study. "If you're thinking about building any sort of device that takes advantage of quantum mechanics, you're going to need to know its [wave function's] parameters really well," he emphasizes.

This includes the wave function's so-called phase, a fully imaginary parameter that is nonetheless often crucial for designing quantum computers. "What has been characterized for a long time is the energies [of the electrons]. That's the basis for all electronics," says Mackillo Kira, a physicist at the University of Michigan, who read an earlier draft of the study but was not directly involved in the work. "But now, with quantum information technology, the next level is to go beyond that and eventually get these [wave function] phases."

To make it to that next level, the team used two lasers and the semiconductor material gallium arsenide. Their experiment consisted of three steps: First, they hit the electrons inside the material with a pulse of near-infrared laser light. This gave those particles extra energy so they would start to quickly race through the semiconductor. When each negatively charged electron started its race, a so-called hole, something like its shadow particle–identical to the electron but positively charged–moved with it. Next, the researchers used another laser pulse to tear the hole and the electron apart, then quickly allowed them to reunite–a sort of quantum version of Peter Pan losing his shadow and having it reattached. When the hole and the electron recombined, the extra energy each accumulated while running solo was released as a burst of light.

Ten years ago a team of physicists led by Mark Sherwin of U.C.S.B. noticed something curious about these bursts: their properties were inexplicably sensitive to the properties of the laser pulses that started the particle run in the first place. Sherwin and his colleagues realized that there was significant and largely unexplored nuance to how a semiconductor's electrons react to light. "This was unexpected," he recalls. "But we decided to explore it further and started systematically looking at it." In the new work, calculations done by postdoctoral scholar Qile Wu, a member of Sherwin's team and co-lead author of the study, proved that this telltale sensitivity is more than a mere curiosity because it can be used to reconstruct the Bloch wave functions of holes in a semiconductor.

The connection between the absorbed laser light and the emitted flash revealed itself in measurements of a property called polarization, or the direction in which light waves oscillate as they travel. In the experiment, the polarization of laser light influenced the phases of the wave functions of the running electrons and of their shadowy partners, the holes. When the reunion of the two produced light at the end of the experiment, the polarization of that flash was determined by these two wave function phases. Because such phases are typically represented as imaginary rather than real numbers in physicists' equations, relating them to the very real and measurable polarization of light was a breakthrough for Wu and his collaborators. Shambhu Ghimire, a physicist at Stanford University, who was not involved with the work, underscores exactly this feature of the new study: it used light to obtain information that was previously seen as purely mathematical. "These [light-based] methods can sometimes be difficult or really conceptually challenging, but most of the time, they provide access to this imaginary part of the complex number [wave function] that you do not have access to with other, conventional methods," he says. Further, the team managed to reverse engineer whole Bloch wave functions from those same polarization measurements.

Ghimire further notes that the kind of laser light the U.C.S.B. researchers used is important beyond its polarization. They employed ultrafast laser pulses, hitting the electrons with light for as little as a trillionth of a second. Electrons in solids tend to bump into atoms instead of moving uninterrupted, so being able to control them with such celerity was crucial for the team to carry out its Peter-Pan-and-his-shadow manipulation of the electron and the hole. Otherwise, in any given run of the experiment, one or the other would likely slam into some atomic obstacle, preventing reunification. Seamus O'Hara, another co-lead author of the study and a Ph.D. student in Sherwin's group, credits some of that technical advantage to the team's use of U.C.S.B.'s state-of-the-art Free-Electron Lasers facility.

But the impact of the work will likely extend beyond specialized facilities and simple semiconductors. In gallium arsenide, Wu's theoretical research showed, very few properties of the reemitted light have to be known for a mathematical reconstruction of Bloch wave functions. Other semiconductor materials may require more complete–and perhaps elusive–knowledge, however. "This work is fascinating as a very fundamental demonstration of something you can do where the answer is really well defined," says Mette Gaarde, a physicist at Louisiana State University, who was also not part of the study. "But the implication is that you could potentially use this to learn something about more complex structures."

The U.C.S.B. team is already making ambitious plans for next steps. Going forward, the researchers are interested in applying their technique to materials in which electrons strongly interact with one another or where laser light would excite particles more exotic than electrons and holes. "We're looking for new materials. If people have semiconductors that they would like to have looked at, we're excited to try," Costello says, eager for more opportunities to glimpse the intangible world of wave functions many more times.

About the Author

Karmela Padavic-Callaghan is an assistant professor at Bard High School Early College Manhattan, where she teaches calculus and physics.

Scientific American vs. the Supernatural

By Katherine Harmon Courage

In 1922 *Scientific American* announced a high-stakes international contest to find scientific proof of ghosts. The competition offered $5,000, and it pitted top scientists of the day against wildly popular psychic mediums. The contest also escalated a growing feud between two famous friends: renowned magician and escape artist Harry Houdini and Sherlock Holmes creator Arthur Conan Doyle.

The magazine's interest in the afterlife was not so much an anomaly but a product of the time. The U.S. and Europe were reeling from enormous numbers of deaths in the Great War and the 1918 influenza pandemic. To their families and friends, the spirits of the newly departed seemed to be appearing everywhere–in parlor séances with mediums and at kitchen tables through store-bought Ouija boards. "There was this desperation, this collective yearning to know if there was existence after death," says David Jaher, whose book *The Witch of Lime Street* chronicles the period.

In parallel to this supernatural fascination, these years were filled with breakneck technological innovation. Electricity and radio were making what was previously unimaginable possible: instant illumination and voices from afar appearing out of thin air. "The science and technology of the time all seemed very magical to people," Jaher says. "There was such a thin line between what is a scientific miracle and what is a supernatural miracle." So cross-Styx communication, or spiritualism, did not seem entirely unreasonable.

In an unlikely turn, Conan Doyle, a trained medical doctor as well as the author behind a famously rational detective, had become one of the highest profile proponents of spiritualism on either side of the Atlantic. He was convinced that, among other things, he had been able to communicate with his dead son. He even toured the U.S. in the early 1920s to lecture on the topic.

On the debunking side was Houdini. The magician and Conan Doyle had briefly been friends, but then the writer tried to arrange for Houdini to receive a message from his dead mother via a medium. The illusionist saw that the act was a ruse, however, and he easily spotted trickery by other mediums as well, such as the use of a wire to move a distant object. He was unhappy with Conan Doyle and condemned the work of mediums as a "racket," Jaher says, "defrauding the bereaved."

Scientific American regularly covered spiritualism as an interest of science. Many well-respected scientists, including renowned physicist Oliver Lodge–a magazine contributor–were vocal defenders of the practice's legitimacy. While in the U.S., Conan Doyle contacted *Scientific American*'s publisher, Orson Munn, and suggested that instead of covering psychic work as an ongoing debate, the magazine ought to take an official stance on it. Munn agreed.

Munn and the magazine's editors decided that the best way to determine their stance would be to hold the aforementioned contest, which was refereed by a committee consisting of two scientists, two psychic experts, and the skeptical Houdini. The contest promised to use the latest scientific tools to ascertain once and for all whether there were true conduits to the spirit world. This equipment included "induction coils, galvanometers, electroscopes, etc., some with the purpose of testing the electrical condition of the medium at the moment when phenomena are produced, others to prove the presence or absence of material objects," the magazine explained in the March 1923 issue.

The psychic tests, initially performed in the magazine's library, got off to a slow and rocky start. Many of Conan Doyle's most revered mediums refused to appear in a public competition. Contestants who did show were quickly dismissed by the judges as tricksters. "I never saw such awkward work in my life," Houdini noted after one of the early sessions.

And so it went, in fits and false apparition starts, for more than a year. Then news began to emerge about a medium in Boston who did not take money for her séances and who seemed to have no particular motive for being a conduit. The woman, Mina Crandon, was married to a respected surgeon and so loathed publicity–unlike other mediums the magazine had encountered–that she received a pseudonym: Margery. So an editor and some of the contest judges set off to the Crandons' residence on Lime Street in Boston for preliminary visits. Bells rang in the dark, a Victrola played without explanation, and the voice of the medium's dead brother conversed with observers.

But Margery could not convince Houdini, who called her "all fraud." The *Scientific American* committee eventually reached the same conclusion after observing nearly 100 séances. In 1925 the magazine announced, "The famous Margery case is over so far as the *Scientific American* Psychic Investigation is concerned."

Notably, however, the publication did not call humbug on the entire field and kept its committee going. As late as 1941, it upped the prize to $15,000. But it seemed unconvinced that conclusive evidence would surface on either side. In a 1942 article, a writer for the magazine mused that "it is, perhaps, too much to hope that it may ever be permanently settled."

About the Author

Katherine Harmon Courage is an award-winning freelance journalist, editor, and author based in Colorado.

Should Scientists Take UFOs and Ghosts More Seriously?

By John Horgan

Like many long-time readers of the New York Times, *I was shocked when the staid old paper published, in 2017, a front-page article on Pentagon investigations of unidentified flying objects, or UFOs. This article, plus a shorter sidebar and a 2019 follow-up, heartened those who believe that extraterrestrials have visited us and annoyed skeptics like my friend journalist Keith Kloor. Last December, I met journalist Leslie Kean, a co-author of the* Times *articles and sole author of the 2010 bestseller* UFOs: Generals, Pilots, and Government Officials Go On the Record, *at a week-long symposium on challenges to conventional scientific materialism, about which I wrote here. At the meeting, which took place at the Esalen Institute in California, Kean talked about the possibility of life after death, a topic she explores in her 2017 book* Surviving Death: A Journalist Investigates Evidence for an Afterlife *(which includes chapters from other contributors). Kean and I hit it off. I told her that, although I have a hard time believing in ghosts and alien visitations, I admire the courage and professionalism with which she investigates these topics. I also enjoy talking to smart people whose views diverge from mine, like renegade biologists Rupert Sheldrake and Stuart Kauffman. So last week, after the* Times *published yet another UFO story by Kean and her collaborator Ralph Blumenthal–which triggered more pushback from Kloor–I emailed Kean a few questions. – John Horgan*

Horgan: When I was a kid, I was obsessed with UFOs and the paranormal. Were you like that too?

Kean: No, not until I was an adult. Although I do remember having mystical feelings about Santa Claus as a young child. It happened when I saw that my cookies, carefully placed next to the Christmas tree, had been nibbled on by Santa during his visitation into my world the previous Christmas Eve. It was solid evidence that something magic, something "supernormal" had actually occurred. This fantastical being who could be everywhere at once had been in my living room and left behind a physical bite mark to prove his existence. The authorities of the day, my parents, confirmed it. I felt momentarily transported, expanded, into a new level of connection to something big and mysterious. That may sound silly, but it was true. When I found out the truth about Santa later, I felt betrayed. Something precious had been taken away. My parents weren't trustworthy because they lied to me. Maybe at some unconscious level this led me to want to find out what's real and to prove the so-called authorities wrong. I'm not totally serious, but I suppose it's possible.

Horgan: When and why did you first decide to write about UFOs? Was there any particular triggering event?

Kean: My serious interest in UFOs as a journalist began in 1999 when I was working as an on-air host and producer for public radio and publishing as a freelancer. I unexpectedly received an explosive 90-page report titled *UFOs and Defense: What Should We Prepare For?* by retired French generals, police, scientists, and an admiral. The report intended to "strip the UFO phenomenon of its irrational layer." The group had spent three years documenting official military and aviation UFO cases. Most stunning was their conclusion: that the "extraterrestrial hypothesis" was the most valid and logical one to explain the data. Of course there was no proof, only an hypothesis. The authors were concerned about the national security implications of the phenomenon and proposed that pilots be trained on how to respond to UFOs to avoid future mishaps or even dangerous accidents. Given the stature and credibility of the group, I thought this was a huge story. I published a lengthy article based on the report, known as the COMETA Report, for the *Boston Globe* in May 2000, which required overcoming the reservations of a very nervous editor. That's what set me on this path, and there was no turning back. And two decades later, I can hardly believe how things have changed.

Horgan: One admirer of your book *UFOs* describes you as an "agnostic" on whether UFOs are actually piloted by aliens. When I met you at Esalen, you struck me as a believer, not an agnostic. Am I wrong?

Kean: Piloted by aliens? I have an open mind, but no, I don't believe that and have never said that. But I also will not rule it out. There are many possibilities on the table. I have made the point over and over that we do not know what these objects are, and that's where things stand. My book concluded that a phenomenon exists, without question, named "unidentified flying objects" by the U.S. Air Force in the 1950s. It's physical, and well documented, even by our government. But what these objects are is another question. That's what everyone wants to know, and that desire has led to all kinds of speculation. On that question my 2010 book was agnostic, and it was recognized as such. These flying machines, whatever they are, might not even have any drivers at all for all we know.

Horgan: What is the best single piece of evidence that UFOs have an extraterrestrial origin?

Kean: The extremely advanced technology that the objects have displayed since the 1950s. They demonstrate tremendous speed and accelerations, the ability to make sharp right-angle turns, stand still in midair, zoom off and disappear in the blink of an eye, and operate under water. They appear to defy the laws of aviation as we know it, since they have no wings or visible means of propulsion. The documentation goes back more than 60 years, when no one on this planet had technology like this. In some cases, experts, such as officials from the French Space Agency, had enough data to rule out all conventional explanations (meaning it wasn't something natural or man-made). These cases represent only a small fraction of those reported, but they are the ones that matter. So, what are we left with?

Horgan: What's your view of alien abduction experiences?

Kean: I find them fascinating and don't know what to make of them. I know sane, intelligent people who report such events, and some even have physical evidence of them. Their lives have been turned upside down by these experiences. However, this is not something I have studied in-depth and it has never been the focus of my work as a reporter. I don't feel qualified to draw conclusions about it. It points to the greater complexity of this issue, which goes beyond any simple hypothesis.

Horgan: Journalist Keith Kloor, writing in *WIRED*, calls your recent *New York Times* article on UFOs "thinly-sourced and slanted." Astrophysicist Katie Mack, in *Scientific American*, says she doesn't take alien spaceships seriously enough to debunk them. How do you respond to these critics?

Kean: People are entitled to their opinions. As one of three people writing the *Times* stories, which include scrutiny by fact-checkers and multiple editors, I simply don't agree with Kloor's statement. We stand by all our reporting at the *New York Times* and will continue to cover the topic whenever we can. Our first story in Dec. 2017 reverberated around the world and has made the subject respectable for many who would not have touched it before. It opened the door to classified briefings on the Hill and a chain of events involving the Navy issuing new reporting guidelines and acknowledging the anomalies in the videos.

I don't think Katie Mack and I stand that far apart. She writes, "It's not that we don't think aliens exist. To the best of my knowledge, most of us do." But the leap to alien spaceships in our atmosphere is another matter, for many reasons which she spells out. I respect her position. I have never claimed that UFOs are alien spaceships. Unfortunately, this is the takeaway for many people from our stories in the *Times*, even though this is not what is actually written and even though we include counter statements to this idea. So I would respond to Katie Mack that any question about alien spaceships misses the point. These are unknowns, plain and simple. But they are physically real. They interact with military pilots and commercial aircraft. Therefore, they deserve investigation.

Horgan: Why did you write *Surviving Death*? Did your own paranormal experiences attract you to this topic?

Kean: During the ten years I was investigating UFOs, I had been intrigued by the question of the possible survival of consciousness when we die. I had poked around into some of the research, especially the work of Ian Stevenson at the University of Virginia studying young children with verified past life memories. After completing work with a film company on a History Channel special based on my book, my publisher (Crown/Random House) invited me to write a second book. Before they made that invitation, I had just completed a draft of a proposal for a book on evidence for possible survival after death, and had planned to give it to my literary agent the very week that they contacted her. It was an amazing synchronicity.

So, it wasn't so much my own experiences that drew me to this, it was my interest in learning more and synthesizing the best, most rigorous material into one volume for the general reader, sort of like I had done for *UFOs*. This was another big mystery facing human beings: what happens when we die? It was the natural topic for me to pursue next, and it was a much bigger challenge than UFOs. Most of my "paranormal" experiences occurred during the time I was involved in the research, which began in 2012. I opened a door and didn't know where it would take me. The experiences I had were beyond my imagination. They were life-changing. Some of them were precipitated by the sudden death of my younger brother in early 2013, a tragedy that deepened my quest for personal answers, as well as intellectual ones. So writing *Surviving Death* was a journey of discovery that unfolded while I was writing it, whereas *UFOs* represented a culmination of ten years of investigation without me ever seeing a UFO. The two books turned out to be very different as a result.

Horgan: Do you ever worry that your claims about life after death will discredit your claims about UFOs, or vice versa?

Kean: Yes, I was worried about that question regarding the material in *Surviving Death*. However, I didn't make any "claims about life after death" that I felt could discredit me, at least in terms of reporting on research and drawing conclusions. I invited others to write their own chapters, and they said things that I didn't say. My conclusion was that the evidence was suggestive, but not definitive, and I never claimed that we survive death. I pointed out that we all have our own criteria for "evidence," which is strongly impacted by personal experience.

I "tested" mental mediumship, received what appeared to be after-death communications from my brother, saw an apparition, and experienced genuine physical mediumship. I thought about whether to make myself vulnerable by including these things. But I think my narrative would have remained one-dimensional and abstract without this personal element. So, I stepped inside this investigation through first-hand examination, and not just from the perspective of a detached observer who studies data and peers into a strange world from the outside. Yes, it could be professionally risky to expose these very personal events, but I felt it was my obligation to do so. It would have been dishonest to omit them, because they impacted my thinking and my effort to come to terms with many remarkable phenomena. However, I was also careful to step back from them, remaining as analytical and discriminating as I was with everything else. The tricky aspect lies in the interpretation of the extraordinary events, not in their reporting.

So far, I have not felt that my work on UFOs has been discredited by my more recent endeavors. I approached *Surviving Death* with journalistic rigor, and this is its strength.

Horgan: When we discussed ghosts and other supernatural phenomena at Esalen, you seemed to be a believer, not an agnostic. Can you clarify your position?

Kean: It depends what you mean by a believer. Paranormal phenomena exist. People have capabilities and experiences that have been labeled "paranormal." They seem to operate outside the limits of the current materialistic framework adapted by most scientists, while at the same time, nobody can explain what consciousness actually is. So the existence of "paranormal phenomena" is not a matter of belief. I find it astonishing that there are still some scientists who adapt the position that it can't be, therefore it isn't. I don't have that choice, because I have witnessed many paranormal phenomena myself, and I know they exist. Those who don't want to believe these things will dismiss them no matter what they read, and they are unlikely to open themselves up to their own encounters with these phenomena.

I think believing comes into play when one tries to establish what the phenomena are, how they work, where they are generated from, why they occur–when addressing the bigger question of what they mean. Beliefs can operate on both sides of the spectrum, from extreme, black and white denial, as we see in so many skeptics, to extreme belief in an afterlife involving claimed "direct knowledge." In fact, none of us knows very much about these big mysteries.

Horgan: What is the best evidence you've seen for life after death?

Kean: That is a huge question. The evidence that I have pulled together in *Surviving Death* comes from so many places, historical and contemporary, experiential and scientific. It's the full gestalt that provides the best evidence. I think cases of very young children who report accurate details of a past life, complete with nightmares about the previous death and knowledge from the previous career, are compelling when the memories can be verified and the previous person is identified. If one does not accept rebirth as an explanation, then something else very "paranormal" is going on. Cases of responsive apparitions are also interesting–these "forms" demonstrate intelligence by reacting to multiple human observers, and sometimes provide information through telepathy about their lives on earth which are verified to be true. There are "actual-death" experiences, as resuscitation scientist Sam Parnia calls them, involving patients who are "dead" yet still return, even after spending hours as a corpse. Mediumship can also be evidential, especially when accurate information is provided that is not known to the recipient but is verified later by a family member. Even if this is a result of the medium's own psychic abilities and does not involve communications from dead people, this is extraordinary in itself. The famous trance medium Mrs. Leonora Piper was studied by experts all over the world, including Willam James. In her sittings, scientists and other discriminating sitters had extensive conversations with their deceased friends and family.

Drop-in communicators, who show up unexpectedly within a physical séance with no connection to any of the sitters or the medium, provide strong evidence for survival. In two famous cases, these communicators, who spoke through the entranced medium, provided detailed information about their lives on earth that were later verified. In the case of the Icelandic medium Indridi Indridason, the communicator spoke in a language unknown to the medium and provided the name Emil Jensen. Jensen's identity was verified decades later by psychologist Erlendur Haraldsson, after searching through records in Copenhagen.

There is a wealth of literature on all of this, and much more evidence. And I like to refer to the words of William James: "If you wish to upset the law that all crows are black, you mustn't seek to show that all crows are black; it is enough if you prove one single crow to be white." Everyone has to find their own white crow.

Horgan: In *Surviving Death*, you say "there are still aspects of Nature that are neither understood or accepted, even though their reality has profound implications for understanding the true breadth of the human psyche and its possible continuity after death." I wholeheartedly agree with this statement, and yet I am, I confess, skeptical of claims about alien visitations and life after death. Am I simply close-minded? Do you ever worry that you are too open-minded?

Kean: You're not closed-minded. Skepticism is a good thing. I too am skeptical about claims of alien visitations as being the simplistic answer to the UFO question. I was a skeptic about the afterlife when

I began my work on that topic; it was my personal experiences that opened my eyes. I don't know how many paranormal events you have witnessed or experienced that might have been totally baffling to you. But I know you have studied consciousness and related phenomena for years, and your skepticism is true for you, and who I am to judge that? Can one be too open-minded? Or are you talking about gullibility? I think I'm grounded, and good at discrimination. Ultimately conclusions about my approach are up to my readers and those who know my work.

Horgan: Are there any pop-culture shows on UFOs and/or the paranormal that you especially like? Dislike?

Kean: I dislike most of the ones I've watched, but there are many that I haven't seen. I loved the movies *Close Encounters of the Third Kind*, and M. Night Shyamalan's *Unbreakable*. I enjoyed the *X-files* until it veered too much away from UFOs and into monsters and freakier territory. I didn't like the History Channel series *Project Blue Book*, premiering in early 2019, because of its distortions and ridiculous plot lines. Ralph Blumenthal and I critiqued that show for the *New York Times* and reported on the real story of Project Blue Book, the Air Force project investigating UFOs in the 50s and 60s. One of my favorite UFO movies was *Unidentified Flying Objects*, made in 1956, with some real people as themselves, which accurately reflected the Blue Book files at the time. I suspect younger people will think this is lame! But that movie was true to fact. *Surviving Death* is the basis for a six-part documentary series that will air this fall on a major streaming platform, so I guess it will become part of pop-culture.

Horgan: Are there any other topics, besides UFOs and life after death, that you think scientists and journalists should take more seriously?

Kean: It's not so much "life after death" because that is not something science could ever definitely prove. It's more about questions around the nature of human consciousness and its manifestations that appear to transcend the limitations of the brain, like a crossing over from the unseen world to that of the seen. Who are we really? Biological robots, or something else? I think all aspects of "superhuman" functioning–precognition, clairvoyance, telepathy, psychokinesis, and energy healing–should be taken seriously. They have been well documented. Where is the curiosity among scientists about the mysteries of the unknown? The challenge they provide to the status quo should make their study even more compelling! Sadly, it's the opposite. I would also love to see more attention paid to mediumship, in all its forms, although I recognize this is not something that can be easily studied in the laboratory. More surveys on near-death experiences could be conducted, along with end-of-life experiences that occur within hospices. Some "parapsychologists" and other scientific investigators are doing brilliant work on all of this, but they are hampered by the mainstream scientific community's irrational disrespect. Someday that dam will break.

About the Author

John Horgan directs the Center for Science Writings at the Stevens Institute of Technology. His books include The End of Science, The End of War *and* Mind-Body Problems, *available for free at mindbodyproblems.com. For many years, he wrote the popular blog Cross Check for* Scientific American.

If Bigfoot Were Real

By Darren Naish

You will, I'm sure, have heard of the unconfirmed North American primate vernacularly termed Bigfoot or Sasquatch.

I have a long-term, unshakeable interest in Bigfoot, and I've thought about the subject quite a lot, at least some of these thoughts having appeared here at Tet Zoo over the years. I do not think that the data we have at the moment–this includes tracks, hairs, vocalisations, photos, and the innumerable eyewitness accounts–provides support for the notion that Bigfoot is real, and have come to the conclusion that it is a sociocultural phenomenon: that people are seeing all manner of different things, combining it with ideas, memes, and preconceptions they hold in their minds, and interpreting them as encounters with a monstrous, human-like biped. This contention is explored further in my recently published book, *Hunting Monsters* (Naish 2016) (and, to prove that I have history, there's also Naish [2012]).

And let me say, by the way, that I would *love* to be wrong... I still do hope that Bigfoot is real; that the version of the creature endorsed by Krantz (1999), Bindernagel (1998), and Meldrum (2006) is accurate and valid. But, alas.

Regular readers of Tet Zoo–and of certain of the things I've published (Conway *et al.* 2013, Naish 2014)–will be familiar with the idea that cryptozoology overlaps extensively with speculative zoology. Bigfoot might not be a genuine undiscovered primate species (so far as we can tell, right now)... but what if it was? In this article, and perhaps in one or two others that might appear in future, I'd like to play a game and ponder things pertaining to the Bigfoot evidence, such as it is. It is, after all, great fun to wonder what the existence of Bigfoot would mean for field biology and ecology in North America, for conservation and wildlife management, for our understanding of primate evolution and diversity, and for the relationship we have with the rest of the natural world. I'm not about to write about all of those hypotheticals right now, but, yes, they're entertaining things to think about. In fact, I'd love to see some speculative fiction written along those lines... oh, to be fair, there is some stuff out there like that already: I'm only familiar with Lee Murphy's books.

Incidentally, an interesting thing I've learnt about Bigfoot while writing this article (and others) is that there's scarcely any Bigfoot imagery online that is marked for re-use: everything is protected by copyright and unavailable for free use by others. Make of that what you will. In the interests of making the world a better place, the pictures I created for this article are all released for use via a CC license.

Biologically consistent, homogenous vocalisations would be documented across North America. Bigfoots purportedly make noises, and a standard part of modern Bigfoot lore is that people might be able to "call in" or even communicate with Bigfoots by making wails, screams, roars or howls, or by hitting trees or rocks to make far-carrying percussive whacks, these sounds resembling the noises that are attributed to the creature. What's notable is that these vocalisations are phenomenally diverse: the "Ohio howls," "Samurai chatter," the whoops, whistles, growls, and howls attributed to this animal well exceed what we'd expect for a single animal species that communicates over long distances, and there's nothing approaching homogeneity of the sort present across known primate species.

Indeed, some of the most incredible of these sounds–if you've never heard the "Sierra sounds" or "Samurai chatter" recorded by Ron Morehead, well, you're in for a treat–sound *nothing at all* like the others that have been reported and recorded, *and* have only been heard exclusively in one small area. Even allowing for the possibility of regional and local dialects, of ontogenetic, annual or seasonal variation, or of this diversity being linked to a diversity of functional roles (close communication vs long-distance communication, mating calls vs parental vocalisations and so on), the noises and calls are absolutely all over the place and not in the least bit homogenous from one region to the next, as they should be if we're dealing with an unknown primate species.

The conclusion must be that the noises have diverse origins, by which I mean that they are mostly sounds made by known animal species, including cattle, coyotes (and their hybrids), and humans. And, yes, I think that many of the more incredible Bigfoot sounds–"Sumarai chatter" and other speech-like utterances among them–were generated by people.

Bigfoot tracks would be easy to find by people who know what they're doing. If Bigfoot is super-rare (as some, though not all, proponents argue that it is), it might follow that its tracks would be rarely encountered and hard to find. That seems reasonable. But the fact is that people who actually track known animal species in a professional or technical capacity are near-universally of the opinion that Bigfoot is not a real animal: (1) they, and their colleagues, don't find evidence for it themselves, and (2) the evidence they have seen is fraudulent or unconvincing. Note that even some of Bigfoot's most noted investigators–I'm thinking of the late René Dahinden–never found tracks themselves.

For a large, ground-dwelling mammal that leaves conspicuous tracks and supposedly occurs continent-wide, Bigfoot is unrealistically cryptic; if it were real, biologists would be at least occasionally finding and reporting its tracks, at at least the same frequency as they do the tracks of such mammals as wolverines, jaguars, pumas, and ocelots, all of which are extremely rare and even of controversial status within certain parts of the USA. The fact that Bigfoot tracks are not found by people trained and with the expertise to do so is a red flag. I'm sorry if this sounds elitist; even if it does, that doesn't stop it from being true.

Bigfoot tracks would be more "biological." A little-discussed aspect of the many Bigfoot tracks on record is that they're decidedly... clean. Yes, there are some famous examples that feature what look like scars and dents, plus there are the infamous Bossburg "cripple foot" tracks... all of which are of doubtful origin and are associated with individuals widely thought—even by proponents—to be hoaxers. But even leaving those aside, the remaining tracks are weird.

A famous sequence of tracks from Bossburg, Washington State, were supposedly made by a Bigfoot with a malformed left foot. The tracks were generally found alongside a road and could be linked to a source considered unreliable even by Bigfoot proponents.

They typically look so neat, so clean. The toes are all too frequently neatly placed together in close contact, and the sole and ball of the foot are smooth and mostly featureless. What I'm getting at is that these don't look like real animal tracks, as they should if Bigfoot were real. In a primate with a human-like foot—especially an enormously big, heavy, bipedal one—the toes should consistently splay apart, as they do in people who go their lives without shoes. And, based on the appearance of wild-living primate feet (humans included), shouldn't Bigfoot have soles that are gnarly, rough, cracked, wrinkled, and fissured? As it is, the soles and balls of Bigfoot tracks look like those of domestic humans who have never walked barefoot outdoors, let alone an animal that lives in forests and mountains, endures freezing outdoor conditions, and walks routinely on rough terrain.

All too many Bigfoot prints are unrealistically "tidy," with closely packed (not spreading), tidily parallel toes and clean, featureless soles. They look to be modelled on the feet of domestic, shoe-wearing humans, not on wild-living primates.

I'm not commenting here on dermal ridges or the alleged mid-tarsal break: neither stand up as evidence supporting the reality of Bigfoot. I discussed both in my recent book (Naish 2016).

There would be Bigfoot DNA all over the place. Anyone who knows anything about Bigfoot knows that there have been several recent claims concerning the discovery of Bigfoot DNA. So far, none have panned out. In the best known study—the one led by Melba Ketchum, published in a paywalled journal created solely to carry the study itself—Bigfoot was reported to be some sort of hybrid between

Homo sapiens and an unidentified second species. The results were widely discussed and derided by qualified working geneticists who showed how the genetic results seemed to mix human with that of other mammals, dogs and bears among them. None of the sequences could be taken to support the hybridisation hypothesis integral to the conclusions. And some geneticists are on record as describing the manuscript as "utter nonsense."

A popular idea in some sectors of the Bigfoot community is that the value and quality of the Ketchum study was played down by cowardly scientists and journal editors who didn't have the balls or integrity to see it get fair treatment. Indeed Ketchum herself wrote of witnessing gross bias, and even referred to the "Galileo Effect." In fact, the Ketchum study–which was submitted to several top-end journals prior to eventual publication–was treated thoroughly and ethically, and found wanting for the reasons mentioned above.

Anyway, my primary point here is that DNA that can't be explained other than by the existence of an unknown distinct primate has not been documented, whereas it would be present all over the place if Bigfoot were real, even if it were an unusual sub-population of *Homo sapiens*. And those of you thinking that this is a dumb thing to say in view of the absence or rarity of alleged Bigfoot remains should note that the collection and examination of eDNA–that is, residual DNA collected from the environment (yes, from water, ice, and sediment)–is now widespread and commonplace.

The main takehome from what I've said here–and I'm repeating what many other scientists have said before me–is that an awful lot of good evidence would have been documented by now if Bigfoot were real. As interesting and intriguing as all those eyewitness reports are, we are simply not seeing the evidence we should, nor is the evidence we have at all convincing. So... why is that?

About the Author

Darren Naish is a science writer, technical editor, and paleozoologist (affiliated with the University of Southampton, UK). He mostly works on Cretaceous dinosaurs and pterosaurs but has an avid interest in all things tetrapod. His publications can be downloaded at darrennaish.wordpress.com. He has been blogging at Tetrapod Zoology since 2006. Check out the Tet Zoo podcast at tetzoo.com!

Section 2: The Making of a Monster

Ghost Lusters: If You Want to See a Specter Badly Enough, Will You?

By Adam Marcus

Most scientists dismiss the vast majority of ghost sightings as hoaxes. But researchers in Canada, England, and elsewhere are exploring what happens in the brain to create the illusion that something is "haunted." So far, they have found evidence that some apparitions may be brain benders caused by spiking EMFs (electromagnetic fields), and possibly even extremely low-frequency sound waves (known as infrasound) so subtle that the ear does not register them as noise.

EMFs emitted by power lines and towers, clock radios, and other electrical sources may help debunk myths that people or things are haunted, says Michael Persinger, a neuroscientist at Laurentian University in Sudbury, Ontario, Canada, who has conducted research on the topic. One such study, published in 2001 in *Perceptual and Motor Skills*, chronicles the experiences of a teenager who in 1996 claimed to be receiving nocturnal visits–one sexual–from the Holy Spirit. The 17-year-old girl, who had sustained mild brain damage at birth, said she also felt the presence of an invisible baby perched on her left shoulder.

When Persinger and his colleagues investigated (at the behest of the girl's mother), they found an electric clock next to the bed that was about 10 inches (25.4 centimeters) from where she placed her head when she slept. Tests showed that the clock generated electromagnetic pulses with waveforms similar to those found to trigger epileptic seizures in rats and humans. When the clock was removed, the visions stopped. Persinger determined that the clock, in combination with the girl's brain injury, were highly likely to have been contributing factors to the perceived nocturnal visits.

Although Persinger believes this case and others to offer compelling evidence that EMFs contribute to a person's perception that something is haunted, experiments intended to prove this theory leave room for doubt.

Christopher French, a psychologist at Goldsmiths, University of London College in London who studies the paranormal, is one researcher who has conducted experiments to test the EMF theory but has been unable to prove its validity. He and colleagues four years ago built a "haunted" room in a London apartment rigged with electromagnetic sources and infrasound generators. They invited 79 volunteers, recruited via the Internet, to spend some time inside the cool, dimly lit space.

Researchers disclosed to the subjects that they might experience some weirdness–feel a presence, tingling, or other strange sensation–while in the room and were given psychological evaluations to assess their susceptibility to the suggestion of the paranormal. This included the Australian Sheep-Goat Scale, which tries to separate likely believers (sheep) from skeptics (goats). Examples of items on the scale include questions about belief in life after death and whether a subject has ever experienced an episode of precognition.

The researchers used a computer to drive twin coils, hidden behind the walls of the room, that generated EMF pulses up to 50 microteslas (a unit for measuring the strength of a magnetic field) of electromagnetic pulses, many times greater than the one-to -four microteslas generated by Persinger's clock. They also used a computer to pump in extremely low-frequency infrasound waves that were well below what humans could possibly hear. Such sounds have been linked, albeit tenuously, to some alleged hauntings. In a 1998 *Journal of the Society for Psychical Research* article entitled "The Ghost in the Machine," Coventry University (U.K.in England) researchers Vic Tandy and Tony Lawrence describe an experiment during which they detected an infrasound wave with a frequency of 18.9 hertz in a factory where workers had reported strange experiences they believed to be paranormal (French and his team used waveforms of 18.9 and 22.3 hertz.).

French's volunteers were exposed to electromagnetic pulses, infrasound, both, or neither. "Most people reported at least some slightly odd sensation, such as a presence or feeling dizzy, and some reported terror, which we hadn't expected," French says. "Terror is obviously quite an extreme reaction, and we only anticipated getting reports of mildly anomalous sensations in the context of this particular experiment." Still, French and his colleagues could not conclude that EMFs played a role in conjuring these feelings.

Like any dutiful researcher, French—who became interested in paranormal psychology after reading the 1981 book *Parapsychology: Science or Magic?*, by the renowned doubter and British psychologist James E. Alcock—has gone into the field, visiting purportedly haunted houses, which are in ample supply in England. He says believers "psych each other up. Sitting in pitch darkness you hear noises, which are common in these old houses, but believers see and hear things that just aren't there, according to our recording devices."

French's findings were published in the journal *Cortex* this month, and he and his colleagues have been trying to garner funding for a follow-up study. It will not be easy—poking holes in ghost stories might appear on its face to be of little scientific value. Still, French insists such research can reveal important truths about the human mind, including questions of memory and delusions. "Within psychology, people talk about reality monitoring, trying to understand how we make distinctions between mental events and events that take place out there in the real world," he says. "It's something we take for granted: Did you really lock the door before you went to bed, or did you just think about it?" On the extreme is schizophrenia, in which the brain makes no distinction between the real and the imagined.

"There's a continuum, and this kind of framework is useful when you're talking about hallucinatory experiences," French says. "People are mistaking their attribution, feeling a product of their own mental processes as something that's taking place in the real world. Anything that can lead to making your mental events more similar to events that take place—a vivid imagination, for example—will make it more difficult to distinguish between the two."

Of course, believers say French cannot see or hear ghosts because he is a "horrible skeptic," which he readily admits. "I wish it was a bit more spooky," he says of his time waiting for apparitions to appear in dank, musty castles. "I'm sitting in the dark, in the cold. I wish something more would happen."

Persinger commends French's team on its "splendid experiment," even if it didn't validate his ideas. Still, he contends, EMFs do affect the body in many ways–from the brain to individual cells, to enzymes, and even DNA. The key to testing their effects on brain activity, he says, is to make sure that the fields are neither too strong nor too weak, and that they come in the right pattern. So he is not willing to give up on finding a way to prove scientifically that EMFs are behind at least some ghost sightings. "I'm a scientist," Persinger says. "I don't believe in anything."

Ghost Stories: Visits from the Deceased

By Vaughan Bell

Carlos Sluzki's cat died a while ago now, but he still sometimes visits. Now more of a shadow cat, the former pet seems to lurk at the edges of Sluzki's vision, as a misinterpreted movement amid the everyday chaos of domestic life. All the same, the shadow cat is beginning to slink away and Sluzki notes that as the grief fades his erstwhile friend is "erasing himself from the world of the present and receding into the bittersweet world of the memories of the loved ones."

The dead stay with us, that much is clear. They remain in our hearts and minds, of course, but for many people they also linger in our senses–as sights, sounds, smells, touches, or presences. Grief hallucinations are a normal reaction to bereavement but are rarely discussed, because people fear they might be considered insane or mentally destabilised by their loss. As a society we tend to associate hallucinations with things like drugs and mental illness, but we now know that hallucinations are common in sober healthy people and that they are more likely during times of stress.

A Common Hallucination

Mourning seems to be a time when hallucinations are particularly common, to the point where feeling the presence of the deceased is the norm rather than the exception. One study, by the researcher Agneta Grimby at the University of Goteborg, found that over 80 percent of elderly people experience hallucinations associated with their dead partner one month after bereavement, as if their perception had yet to catch up with the knowledge of their beloved's passing. As a marker of how vivid such visions can seem, almost a third of the people reported that they spoke in response to their experiences. In other words, these weren't just peripheral illusions: they could evoke the very essence of the deceased.

Occasionally, these hallucinations are heart-rending. A 2002 case report by German researchers described how a middle aged woman, grieving her daughter's death from a heroin overdose, regularly saw the young girl and sometimes heard her say "Mamma, Mamma!" and "It's so cold." Thankfully, these distressing experiences tend to be rare, and most people who experience hallucinations during bereavement find them comforting, as if they were re-connecting with something of the positive from the person's life. Perhaps this reconnecting is reflected in the fact that the intensity of grief has been found to predict the number of pleasant hallucinations, as has the happiness of the marriage to the person who passed away.

There are hints that the type of grief hallucinations might also differ across cultures. Anthropologists have told us a great deal about how the ceremonies, beliefs, and the social rituals of death differ greatly across the world, but we have few clues about how these different approaches affect how people experience the dead after they have gone. Carlos Sluzki, the owner of the shadow cat and a cross-cultural researcher at George Mason University, suggests that in cultures of non-European origin the distinction between "in here" and "out there" experiences is less strictly defined, and so grief hallucinations may not be considered so personally worrying. In a recent article, he discussed the case of an elderly Hispanic lady who was frequently "visited" by two of her children who died in adulthood and were a comforting and valued part of her social network. Other case reports have suggested that such hallucinations may be looked on more favorably among the Hopi Indians, or the Mu Ghayeb people from Oman, but little systematic work has been done.

And there, our knowledge ends. Despite the fact that hallucinations are one of the most common reactions to loss, they have barely been investigated and we know little more about them. Like sorrow itself, we seem a little uncomfortable with it, unwilling to broach the subject and preferring to dwell on the practicalities—the "call me if I can do anything," the "let's take your mind off it," the "are you looking after yourself?"

Only a minority of people reading this article are likely to experience grief without re-experiencing the dead. We often fall back on the cultural catch all of the "ghost" while the reality is, in many ways, more profound. Our perception is so tuned to their presence that when they are not there to fill that gap, we unconsciously try to mold the world into what we have lived with for so long and so badly long for. Even reality is no match for our love.

About the Author

Vaughan Bell is visiting professor in the Department of Psychiatry at the Universidad de Antioquia, Medellín, Colombia. He blogs at Mindhacks.

How Chasing Bigfoot Can Lead to Actual Science

By Alison Gilchrist

As a biologist in a lab studying how monkeys and other primates are related, I've become fascinated with Bigfoot. Often described and portrayed as half man, half ape, Bigfoot (if it exists) could represent a possible link in the evolution of humans from our primate ancestors. Bigfoot also represents the realm of the unknown, the undiscovered. Rumors from all over the world about sightings of Bigfoot, Sasquatch, and yeti tantalizingly hint that there are mythical creatures just waiting to be discovered.

So, the story of Charlotte Lindqvist and her own brief experience with the Bigfoot mythology caught my attention. Lindqvist was probably the last person to expect a call about shadowy creatures rumored to live in Tibet. She's a geneticist at the University at Buffalo in New York–quite a long way from the Himalayas–and she studies bears.

But in 2013 a documentary production company, Icon Films, wanted to find out whether the creatures known as yeti (or Bigfoot or Sasquatch) really existed, and they thought Lindqvist could help. The company had collected samples of fur and bone in the Himalayas, and Lindqvist had the technology to determine whether they came from a familiar animal or one unknown to science.

"I saw my opportunity to get hold of some samples that would otherwise be very hard to get," she says.

Lindqvist didn't believe that the samples were from mysterious yetis. Instead, she suspected that the samples were from bears–similarly large and hairy, but not mysterious at all.

"Bears in the Himalayan region and Tibetan Plateau are fairly elusive. We don't know much about them, and the Himalayan brown bear is endangered," says Lindqvist.

So, she said yes, she'd analyze the DNA. She knew that she could identify bear DNA and that the DNA of a mysterious monster wouldn't look like any animal previously analyzed. In that case she would have discovered an entirely new species.

Although the film production company might have been hoping to pinpoint the elusive mythological beast, Lindqvist's instincts turned out to be correct. For the most part, the samples were from bears. Specifically, they were from Tibetan brown bears, an Asian black bear, and a Himalayan brown bear. From bits of hair and bone, Lindqvist was able to sequence the bears' mitochondrial DNA.

Usually, when we talk about DNA, we're talking about DNA from the cell nucleus. Mitochondrial DNA is different from the genetic code that makes up our 23 chromosomes. It's found in another part of the cell, an energy-producing organ. It's not always good for identifying individuals, but it is good for distinguishing among species.

Mitochondrial DNA is also easier to sequence than the rest of the animal genome because there are more copies of it in each cell. Sure enough, Lindqvist was able to fully sequence the mitochondrial genome of a Himalayan brown bear—the first time that had been achieved.

Lindqvist didn't stop at identifying where the samples came from. Using this full mitochondrial DNA sequence, plus partial sequences from the regular DNA of Tibetan brown bears and an Asian black bear, and information about the geography of the region, Lindqvist concluded that 650,000 years ago, glaciers forced a single population of bears apart, creating two isolated populations. Over time, these populations became the two distinct subspecies—Himalayan brown bears and Tibetan brown bears—that they are today.

This was not the first time that legendary creatures had inadvertently lent a hand to genetics studies. In 2013, a geneticist at Oxford University, Bryan Sykes, also leveraged the yeti frenzy for genetics studies of bears to find the DNA of an animal related to Paleolithic polar bears.

And it doesn't stop with yetis. I was surprised and delighted to find that other creatures of myth will benefit the field of genetics. In 2017, a scientist from New Zealand embarked on a sequencing journey similar to that of Lindqvist. Neil Gemmell, a geneticist at the University of Otago, proposed sequencing DNA from Loch Ness, the lake in Scotland where a well-known mythical sea monster is supposed to live (or to have lived at some point). The project is set to officially start this month, when Gemmell's team will begin collecting water samples.

Gemmell, who studies environmental DNA–the DNA that animals shed in hair, skin, scales, and feces–has never believed in the dinosaur-like sea monster. But he does believe in its ability to get people excited about science. Although some may not have been initially interested in Gemmell's current work in New Zealand, the Loch Ness project is instantly accessible.

"Not that many people are interested in hearing about what we're discovering, but they are interested in the Loch Ness Monster," he says.

Although Gemmell is candid about the fact that he doesn't believe the researchers will discover the elusive sea creature, he still believes the project will yield interesting results and be an influential science communication platform. Sure enough, thanks to the "Nessie" connection, Gemmell's project has already made headlines around the world before it has even begun. "I think it's neat!" he says. "And my kids think it's neat."

Regardless of whether Nessie is found, Gemmell and his research group will gather useful information about the population of creatures present in Loch Ness. He plans to test several hypotheses using sequenced DNA from the lake. "Hypothesis one is that [the Loch Ness monster] is an ancient remnant plesiosaur population or something like that–the so-called Jurassic hypothesis," said Gemmell. "Which, let's be honest, is basically bogus stuff–it's just ridiculous. But nonetheless, we could test that."

He also plans to test whether there is evidence of giant fish, such as sturgeon, or even evidence of sharks occasionally getting into the lake. And while he's testing the water for things that might explain Nessie sightings, he'll also be asking some questions that address different issues. For example, what is the microbial and bacterial diversity like in Loch Ness? And are there invasive species in the lake?

"There's been an awful lot of people taking an awful lot of gear into Loch Ness over the years," said Gemmell. "There's suggestions that there's an invasive shrimp species from the southern United States in Loch Ness. There's been reports recently of pink salmon, which is of course a *Pacific* salmon, in the Ness River."

There are just as many questions about species we know to exist as about species that probably don't exist. Powerful datasets can come out of the search for elusive creatures, whether or not they are real. My fascination with Bigfoot aside, it might be time to start thinking about how we can leverage myths about fairies to study the skies. So, the question now for evolutionary biologists and geneticists alike is: what other mythological creatures can we search for in order to learn more about the less charismatic–but just as magical–creatures on Earth?

About the Author

Alison Gilchrist is a fourth-year Ph.D. candidate at the University of Colorado, Boulder, in the Department of Molecular, Cellular and Developmental Biology.

Here Be Dragons

By Kelly Reidy

Dragons are not new. *Game of Thrones* tells us that they date back to some arguably medieval time, which may or may not predate the adventures of Smaug, the dragon from *The Hobbit*. In the nonfiction world, Christian legend tells of St. George slaying a dragon, and that tale probably derives from pre-Christian stories. Dragons show up in Chinese mythology as well—and in Bhutan, the Druk, or thunder dragon, is emblazoned on the national flag. And in fact, anthropologists have found dragons in art spanning thousands of years and independently created by people from all over the world.

The ubiquity of dragons across time and space may be related to fears inherited from some of humans' most adorable ancestors: vervet monkeys. In his book *An Instinct for Dragons*, David E. Jones cites a study showing that these primates have an innate fear of lions, snakes, and eagles. That's a recipe for a dragon if I've ever heard one! Thus, humans may be evolutionarily predisposed to fear these animals.

But this only leads to more questions: What about the fire-breathing capabilities of European dragons, or the rain-bringing skills of Asian dragons, or the people-eating habits of Maori dragons? And why do some dragons fly while others slither?

The appearance, behavior, and general level of horror of dragons vary wildly across cultures. These differences can tell us something about the natural history of their creators; this is where both local fears and local fauna play a role.

In northern China, around 300 B.C., workers digging a canal came across a fossilized animal skeleton. Remember that the theory of evolution wasn't a thing yet, so people assumed this was the skeleton of an existing creature rather than the extinct nonavian dinosaur that it probably was. It went on record as a dragon skeleton—more fuel for the long-existing fire of Chinese dragon mythology.

Dragons appear in Chinese art from at least as far back as 1100 B.C. These dragons are relatively tame-looking and typically serpentine, with multiple sets of legs and a vaguely lion-like head. They don't have wings, but they can fly. Two ancient Chinese rulers declared themselves to be direct descendent of dragons, and so dragons in many Chinese cultures became symbols of power. Contrary to the gut feeling you might be having right now, these dragons are generally seen as wise and benevolent–heroic, even–bringing rain to dry crops and pretty much saving entire civilizations.

In Europe, on the other hand, dragons are usually the bad guys. European dragon myths feature dragons as vicious monsters whose raison d'être involves getting slain by saints who need hero credibility. St. George, known primarily as a dragon-slayer, is now the patron saint of England and even has his own holiday on April 23.

Appearance-wise, these European dragons are a little wackier than their Asian cousins. They look more like snake/eagle/lion combinations straight out of your worst fever dreams. Usually they have legs and wings and a snake tongue, sometimes fur, sometimes scales, sometimes both. For good measure, they can also breathe fire–the fire-breathing animals in Hieronymus Bosch's delightful Renaissance-era paintings of hell may have been an inspiration for this feature. The very real and very prehistoric-looking Nile crocodile might also have been an influence, as it regularly swam up to European shores from Egypt and traipsed around on land.

Further south, in New Zealand, the *taniwha* are dragon-like creatures from Maori mythology. In this case, take the basic snake/eagle/lion innate-fear combo and add something more local: the great white shark. In fact, the Maori word for great white shark is *mangō-taniwha*. But don't worry too much, as these creatures can be benevolent protectors–sometimes. At other times, they can be totally horrifying people-eaters. As a cherry on top of that nightmare cake, note also that in some stories, *taniwha* have shape-shifting abilities.

After thousands of years of international dragon mythology, you'd be forgiven for thinking that their moment has passed.

But dragons continue to spark our curiosity and captivate our imaginations; today, they make appearances in pop culture via *The Lord of the Rings*, Dungeons & Dragons (and by extension, *Stranger Things*), *Game of Thrones*, and even in band names like *Imagine Dragons* and *DragonForce*.

These pop dragons are mostly European-style in appearance, but their roles are more complex than the traditional Western "set 'em up, knock 'em down" scheme. They run the gamut from the occasionally disagreeable allies in *Game of Thrones* to the well-spoken monster in *The Hobbit*.

Either way, stay vigilant, dear reader, because if *Game of Thrones* has taught us anything, it's that "the night is dark and full of terror."

About the Author

Kelly Reidy is a visiting assistant professor at Pratt Institute. She leads offbeat tours at various museums in New York City, and writes and performs ukulele songs about, among other things, love and mathematics.

The American Fascination with Zombies

By Krystal D'Costa

I think I must be prepared. For what? The impending zombie apocalypse, of course! Surely the plethora of zombie movies, books, survival guides, and even exercise regimens have given me a sense of how to survive in the event of this particular catastrophe. If you've seen even one zombie movie, I'd be willing to bet that you're pretty prepared too. If you haven't, go watch *Zombieland*. It provides a fair list of "rules" that should boost your chances of survival. For example, "When in doubt, know your way out" and "Check the backseat" make a lot of sense. Then again, those might be things you should be doing anyway.

Zombies aren't pretty creatures. Popular media depicts them in assorted states of decay. They shamble. They're insatiable cannibals. And, well, they're dead. So why can't we get enough of them?

Folklore is home to a host of undead characters: mummies, skeletons, vampires, ghouls, and ghosts can be found under one name or another in almost all mythologies. Though closely linked with Vodoun magic and religion, the zombie is no exception: dybbuks, jumbies, djodjos, and duppies all bear some resemblance to the Haitian zombie, which is a composite of African beliefs transported to the Caribbean via the slave trade.[1] Slaves from the Gulf of Guinea transported rites and rituals from the classical East and the Aegean, which took root following Haiti's revolution in 1804.[2] This zombie is a complex creature: though, like its cinematic counterpart it lacks consciousness, it is a much more nuanced and manipulated figure. Anthropologist Wade Davis proposed that the Haitian zombie is a pharmacological product created by a bokor.[3] A powder created from the toxins found in the puffer fish is administered to induce a lethargic sleep from which the afflicted may be roused and controlled. However, analysis of this powder has yielded frustratingly little information: ingredients appear to vary (including human remains, toads, lizards, millipedes, tarantulas, ground glass, and various plants) as does administration. For example, the powder may be strewn over the path frequented by the intended victim, or on his doorstep–this hardly seems very effective. Haitian traditions allow for the possibility of poisoning, but also posit a supernatural origin: a body is buried and resurrected without cause–it is just called by name by a sorcerer and emerges without will, memory, or consciousness, ready to do one's bidding.[4] Typically, it will work for its creator, either performing labor or serving as a guard of some sort, and may be rented or loaned.

This corporeal zombie–distinguished from the spiritual zombie that Vodoun beliefs also permit–is the basis for the Hollywood zombie, which cannot be controlled and is bent on destruction. In both cases, the zombie is a shade of the human from whom it is derived, however the degradation of the latter's former humanity is precisely what makes it horror that we can't turn away from. Much has been written about the metaphors inherent in Hollywood zombies and their ties to capitalism, the Other, and science and technology gone awry.[5, 6] Yet, zombies capture our imagination because they are extensions of what we know to be human–they provide a glimpse into the breakdown of the social order.

Zombies are not meant to be. We engage in systematic mourning and funeral rites to remove the deceased and his remains from our immediate awareness. While we make allowances for the length of the grieving period, we support the bereaved with the belief (even if it is unspoken) that they will eventually cease to mourn as deeply in a visible way. But we also distance ourselves from the dead because they are a reminder of our mortality. They are gone, after all. And not only that, but their bodies begin to decay. Zombies force us to confront these sorts of issues. In death, the social order does not matter:

> *Society's infrastructure begins to break down, especially those systems associated with the government and technology. Law enforcement is depicted as incompetent and backwater (the local sheriff is a stereotyped yokel with a "shoot first" attitude), so people must fend for themselves instead. The media do what they*

> *can, broadcasting tidbits of helpful information and advice by way of the radio and television, but the outlook is fundamentally grim: Hide if you can, fight if you have to. In the end, the rigid structure of society proves little help; human survivors are left to their own devices with no real hope of rescue or support. Motley groups are forced into hiding, holing up in safe houses of some kind where they barricade themselves and wait in vain for the trouble to pass.*[7]

Infectious disease researchers have already determined that in the event of a zombie outbreak, humanity would be up the creek–to put it mildly. In all the models investigated, the collapse of civilization is imminent.[8] All but the most aggressive quarantine strategies would fail, and when the dead can come back to life, well, it means that there is an endless source of recruits waiting to be called forth. Albeit a bit tongue-in-cheek, researchers advise that in the face of a zombie apocalypse, quick, decisive action would be necessary: "the most effective way to control the rise of the undead is to hit hard and hit often."[9]

In these instances, the undead reflect concerns about mortality and social order. Zombies are our creation–whether in the Vodoun tradition or the result of radiation or a viral outbreak, zombies rise because we make it possible for them to do so. But perhaps because they are former human beings, it is hard for us to imagine that society would come completely undone. In recent years, we have seen the rise of a smarter class of the undead, one that can organize. And though that organization seems to make its mission the eradication of "normal" people, these new zombies are more intimidating in that they retain a bit more of their former selves. The film version of *I Am Legend* gives us a class of zombie that is frightening fast, strong, and aggressive. They coordinate attacks and set traps–they can *retaliate*. Stephen King's *The Cell* features undead who are organized around a leader, and begin a process of "turning" normals (rather than simply eating them). These zombies provide a glimpse of the world to come, a world that we may help create–which is perhaps why we just can't turn away.

Referenced

Ackermann, H., & Gauthier, J. (1991). The Ways and Nature of the Zombi *The Journal of American Folklore, 104* (414) DOI: 10.2307/541551

Bishop, K. (2006). Raising the Dead *Journal of Popular Film and Television, 33* (4), 196-205 DOI: 10.3200/JPFT.33.4.196-205

Bishop, K. (2008). The Sub-Subaltern Monster: Imperialist Hegemony and the Cinematic Voodoo Zombie *The Journal of American Culture, 31* (2), 141-152 DOI: 10.1111/j.1542-734X.2008.00668.x

Munz, Philip et al. (2009). When Zombies Attack! Mathematical Modelling of an Outbreak of Zombie Infection. In *Infectious Disease Modelling Research Progress*. JM Tchuenche and C Chiyaka, eds. Nova Science Publishers: pp 133-150. [pdf]

Shaviro, S. (2002). Capitalist Monsters *Historical Materialism*, 10 (4), 281-290 DOI: 10.1163/156920602604744 86

Notes: 1. Ackermann and Gauthier (1991): 489. | 2. Bishop (2008): 143. | 3. Ackermann and Gauthier: 475. | 4. Ackermann and Gauthier: 474. | 5. Bishop (2008). | 6. Shapiro (2002): 77. | 7. Bishop (2006): 202. | 8. Munz, Hudea, Imad et. al. (2009): 146. | 9. Munz: 146.

About the Author

Krystal D'Costa is an anthropologist working in digital media in New York City.

Why We Are So Intrigued by Zombies

By Michael Shermer

The 2014 premier of *The Walking Dead*–AMC's postapocalyptic dystopian television series about zombies–was the most watched cable show in history. There have been a slew of popular zombie films, such as *Dawn of the Dead*, *Day of the Dead*, *Night of the Living Dead*, *28 Days Later*, *I Am Legend* and of course the perennial favorite *Frankenstein*. There is even a neuroscience text on the zombie brain, *Do Zombies Dream of Undead Sheep?* by Timothy Verstynen and Bradley Voytek (Princeton University Press, 2014), in which the authors consider real disorders that could turn the living into the living dead. Why are we so intrigued by zombies?

Zombies, for one thing, fit into the horror genre in which monstrous creatures–like dangerous predators in our ancestral environment–trigger physiological fight-or-flight reactions such as an increase in heart rate and blood pressure and the release of such stress hormones as cortisol and adrenaline that help us prepare for danger. New environments may contain an element of risk, but we must explore them to find new sources of food and mates. So danger contains an element of both fear and excitement.

We also have a fascination with liminal beings that fall in between categories, writes philosopher Stephen T. Asma in his 2009 book *On Monsters* (Oxford University Press). The fictional Frankenstein monster, like most zombies, is a being in between animate and inanimate, human and nonhuman. Hermaphrodites fall between male and female, and hybrid animals fall between species. Our innate templates for categorizing objects and beings are modified through experience, and when we encounter something or someone new, we check for category matches. Moderate deviation from the known category generates attention (friend or foe?), Asma says, but a "cognitive mismatch" elicits both dread and fascination. Add the emotion of disgust triggered by slime, drool, snot, blood, feces and rotting flesh, and we may find ourselves both repelled and drawn to such liminal creatures.

Distinguishing between zombies and nonzombies also hints at the deeper problem of xenophobia, which evolved as part of our nature to be suspicious of outsiders who, in our evolutionary past, were potentially dangerous. People from other groups, especially those perceived to be a threat, are moved into other cognitive categories and relabeled as mongrels, pests, vermin, rats, lice, maggots, cockroaches and parasites—all the easier to destroy them. Such labels are inevitably applied to new outgroups moving into the territory of an established in-group or conflicting economically or culturally with one—blacks moving into white neighborhoods, Jews establishing businesses in gentile-dominated markets, the Hutus resenting the dominant Tutsis in Rwanda. Fundamentalist Muslims do not "hate our freedoms" (as President George W. Bush conjectured). Instead, as Asma notes, they created a uniquely American monster in which "we are seen as godless, consumerist *zombies*, soulless hedonists without honor, family, or purpose."

On our cognitive maps are areas labeled "Here Be Monsters," where we put outsiders perceived to be dangerous. Fortunately, we have learned to curb such chauvinisms. As a result, the moral sphere has expanded to include all racial and ethnic groups as worthy of respect and equality, in principle if not always in practice. We have done so, in part, by overriding our instinctive impulses through reason, allowing us to take the perspective of another. Shakespeare worked out the logic in *The Merchant of Venice* when he has Shylock ask:

> *Hath not a Jew eyes? Hath not a Jew hands, organs, dimensions, senses, affections, passions; fed with the same food, hurt with the same weapons, subject to the same diseases, heal'd by the same means, warm'd and cool'd by the same winter and summer, as a Christian is? If you prick us, do we not bleed? If you tickle us, do we not laugh? If you poison us, do we not die? And if you wrong us, do we not revenge? If we are like you in the rest, we will resemble you in that.*

Perhaps zombies and other fictional beings stimulate those neural regions of our nonzombie brains that allow for a healthy and nonviolent outlet for such ancient callings.

About the Author

Michael Shermer is publisher of Skeptic *magazine (www.skeptic.com). His next book is* The Moral Arc.

Zombie Fever: A Mathematician Studies a Pop Culture Epidemic

By Evelyn Lamb

Zombies. They're everywhere. My dentist and his assistant spent my last visit chatting about *The Walking Dead* while drilling into my head, and it seems like every reasonably large town hosts a zombie run. Science education is getting in on the trend, too. Colleges have classes about zombies, AMC (the network that broadcasts *The Walking Dead*) is sponsoring a free zombie-themed survival course, and Texas Instruments developed an app for teaching neuroscience using ideas from zombie movies. Even the CDC wants to help you prepare for the zombie apocalypse. Frankly, it's a little out of hand. How long will this zombie fever last?

Sarah Reehl, who is now a mathematics graduate student at Utah State University, noticed the ubiquity of zombies while she was working on her undergraduate thesis at Carroll College in Montana last year. "I was watching *The Walking Dead* and trying to make physiologically correct arguments about zombie mechanics. My instincts were to model a real zombie infection," she wrote in an email. But in her search for data about zombie behavior, she decided that zombies were more interesting as a pop culture phenomenon and shifted her focus. In her thesis, Reehl used a standard epidemiological model to study not only seasonal influenza rates but also our culture's obsession with zombies.

Reehl used what is called an SIR model for both influenza and zombie fever. SIR stands for three groups in a population: "susceptible," "infected," and "recovered" or "removed." It is particularly useful for diseases–such as measles, chicken pox, and influenza–that people typically get only once. (Yes, you may have gotten the flu more than once, but you didn't get the same strain every time. Influenza mutates so quickly that long-term immunity is impossible.) In disease modeling, the population consists of people or other organisms, and researchers determine a system of differential equations that represent the likelihood of transmission of the disease and how quickly an epidemic will pass through the population.

"What happens if we try to model popular culture trends as infectious diseases?" Reehl asks in her thesis. With the help of Google's n-gram viewer, she used words instead of people as the population in question. The n-gram viewer is a tool for exploring trends in language. When you search a word (a 1-gram) or phrase (an n-gram, where n is the number of words in the phrase), you get a graph that shows its popularity over time, based on its prevalence in a corpus of books that Google has digitized.

Reehl looked at two past linguistic phenomena, "jitney" and "groovy," to get a feel for the rise and fall of trendy words. Based on this background, she developed an initial guess of a model for "zombie" prevalence, which she then refined. Of course, the devil is in the details, and different assumptions about transmission rates and the susceptibility of the language to the word "zombie" yield different models. Reehl believes that in the most likely model of zombie fever, over the next 25 years, "zombie" will come close to the popularity of Halloween stalwarts "vampire" and "Frankenstein," after which it will gradually subside but not die out completely. But she also thinks it would be interesting to develop a model that would take into account the use of the word "zombie" not only in books but also on Twitter and television, where she thinks zombies might be more popular.

If you, like me, are too squeamish to watch zombie movies and are therefore kind of bored with the trend, it's going to be a while before the last axe settles into the skull of a fictional monster with a hunger for brains. Reehl predicts that zombie fever will peak around the year 2038, but it will probably not return to pre-*Shaun of the Dead* levels until after 2080. Better keep the axe handy.

About the Author

Evelyn Lamb is a freelance math and science writer based in Salt Lake City, Utah.

Section 3: Inside the Minds of Monsters

How Would Immortality Affect a Vampire's Memory?

By Brian Levine

About 30 years ago I saw my first Jim Jarmusch movie, *Stranger than Paradise*, at the Detroit Film Theatre, a popular site for indie film screening situated in the Detroit Institute of Arts. It is fitting that Jarmusch's latest film, *Only Lovers Left Alive*, starring Tom Hiddleston and Tilda Swinton as Adam and Eve, takes place in Motor City.

Being a film about vampires set in city where I once lived, it got me to thinking about what vampires can teach us about the workings of memory. Vampires have two features of interest to memory theorists. First, to the extent that they avoid angry mobs, they are immortal, allowing them to accumulate life experiences indefinitely. Second, they are immune to the effects of aging. This is of interest because, in the living, the deleterious effects of long periods of time on memory are inextricably confounded with the effects of aging on brain structure and function. A vampire's memory would allow us to disentangle the effects of time and aging.

I must admit that I have failed to attract even a single vampire to my laboratory for testing, but in the absence of data, allow me to speculate on how your friendly neighborhood vampire might process memories of events at a specific time or place, beginning with the issue of immortality.

Episodic Memory

If you lived forever, would you remember everything that happened to you? The answer is no. Memory decays exponentially over time. In the following figure, the horizontal axis represents time, starting from the present on the right, going exponentially into the past to the left as the years shrink and collapse upon themselves. The vertical axis represents the percentage of events accessible to recall, also plotted as an exponential function. While you may recall nearly everything that happened today, after three days, this goes down to 10 percent for most people. A month from now, we would be hard pressed recall more than 1 percent of today's events. After a year, a tenth of 1 percent and so on.

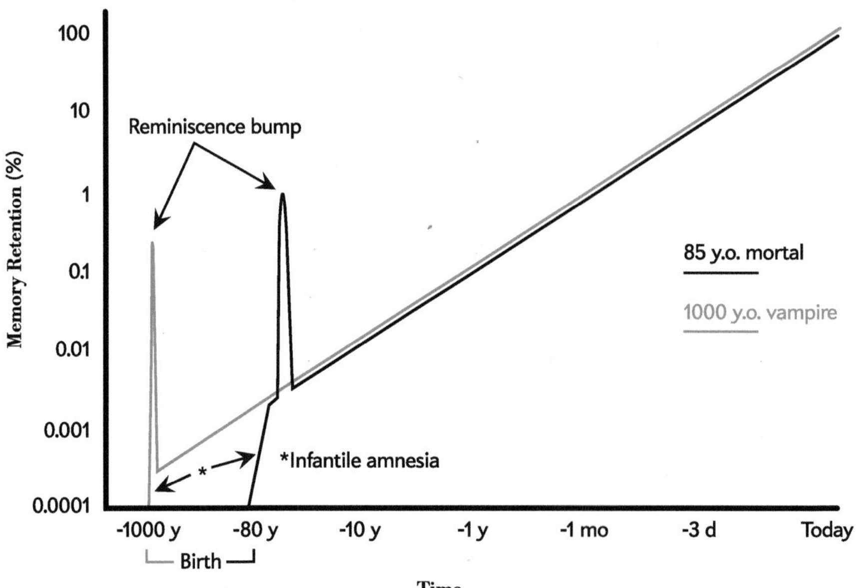

Credit: Brian Levine

With a couple of exceptions, this function is monotonic, meaning that the relationship between time and forgetting is constant in perpetuity. A normal 85-year-old mortal can recall but a scintilla (about 0.003 percent) of daily life events from his or her primary school years. Extrapolating this to a 1,000-year-old vampire, the figure would be 0.0002 percent. This is not necessarily a bad thing; forgetting is a normal process important the formation of new memories. As psychologist Théodule-Armand Ribot stated in 1882, "Without the total obliteration of an immense number of states of consciousness, and the momentary repression of many more, recollection would be impossible." For both mortals and vampires, the most useful memories in terms of daily activities (say remembering where you parked the car or where to find fresh blood) are the most recent ones.

The first exception to the monotonic forgetting function is the period of infantile amnesia from birth to around age four, where few to no events are retained into the adult years. The second is the "reminiscence bump," which refers to the period peaking around age 20 during which events and the cultural milieu are bound up with the formation of one's identity, gracing that period with enhanced recall and preference.

Events occurring during the reminiscence bump survive in memory because they are personally significant and emotional. These same events are also repeatedly recalled and reviewed in memory, enhancing their status in our autobiographies. Vampires were once young, after all, so they too are entitled to a reminiscence bump. There is no reason to think that a vampire's first kiss would fade from memory even after 1,000 years. Thus vampires' early adulthood events would retain their special status in memory, as is the case for mortals.

The previous figure shows the percentage of events recalled, but what about the quality or vividness of those memories? In 2002, my group discovered that with age, mortals recall fewer episodic (specific) details (e.g., "it was a shiny red Mustang") and more non-specific details or commentary (e.g., "they don't make Mustangs like they used to!"). This phenomenon may be due to an age-related failure to suppress off-task thoughts. While vampires' detailed recall may suffer from the passage of time, their stories (such as Adam's personal reminiscences of Lord Byron in *Only Lovers Left Alive*), immune to the effects of aging, would be crisp and free of clutter.

Non-Episodic Memory

Memory of skills, habits, and expertise are not subject to the same decay as the memory of episodes and events. Yet when it comes to self-improvement, the inevitability of death forces certain choices.

Although I would like to pick up a new language or perfect my tempura technique, there are other priorities and there is only so much time.

Vampires are confined to evening hours, but otherwise have a lot of time to work with. Whereas aging shifts mortals' focus towards present well-being and "generativity" (the desire to nurture younger generations) and away from long-term goals, no such effect is expected in vampires. Although some squander their immortality (there is one such example in *Only Lovers Left Alive*), vampires are generally a cultured, even uppity bunch that can hold their own in any conversation. In *Only Lovers Left Alive*, when packing for a trip, Eve selects books in several languages.

With aging, mortals acquire more knowledge and wisdom, yet processing speed and physical capacities decline, leading to the aphorism that youth is wasted on the young. For vampires, there is no theoretical limit on the number of skills that could be acquired to a reasonable level of competence, aside from pastimes that require being outdoors in the daylight or the use of a mirror. Vampires have the best of both worlds: whereas mortals are wise and slow, vampires are wise and fast. The tricky part would be to maintain these learned skills. Having taken piano lessons in the Elizabethan era would not be of much use today without regular practice. The following advice, amalgamated from cognitive neuroscience research, is for readers who are vampires and want to maximize their self-improvement:

1. Choose two or three things from different categories, such as physical skills, artistic talents, and intellectual pursuits (e.g., billiards, playing the banjo, and Greek literature, respectively). The variety of tasks will keep up your motivation and support training-induced neuroplasticity through strengthening of complementary brain systems.
2. Spaced or distributed practice is better than massed practice, so cycle your training for each task across days, allowing for a day or two of rest before returning to each task.

3. Take one or two days a week to reinforce and maintain skills that you have already mastered.
4. Get a good day's sleep, for sleep is essential for consolidation of learned skills.
5. Finally, choose skills with staying power. You'd be sorry if you had chosen macramé in the 70s just because it was hot.

The complexity of the human brain, with 100 billion neurons and 100 trillion connections, is beyond comprehension, at least with current methods. Given sufficient time, the amount of information that could be absorbed through the neuroplastic sculpting of these connections is limitless. The benefits of greater exposure and experience enjoyed by mortals are offset by the liabilities of age-related brain changes. Although vampires are subject to the same forgetting function as mortals, they illustrate the brain's capacities for learning and memory that can only be seen in the absence of brain aging and finite temporal horizons.

About the Author

Brian Levine is a senior scientist at Baycrest's Rotman Research Institute in Toronto and professor of psychology and medicine (neurology) at the University of Toronto. He is a lead investigator on the Baycrest Brain Health in Professional Athletes Study, involving brain and behavior studies of retired professional ice hockey players.

Bigfoot Anatomy

By Marguerite Holloway

One overcast Sunday morning in 1996, Jeffrey Meldrum and his brother drove to Walla Walla, Wash., to see if they could find Paul Freeman, a man renowned in Bigfoot circles as a source of footprint casts. Meldrum–who has followed Bigfoot lore since he was a boy–had heard that Freeman was a hoaxer, "so I was very dubious," he recalls. The brothers arrived unannounced, Meldrum says, and chatted with Freeman about his collection. Freeman said he had found tracks just that morning, but they were not good, not worth casting. The brothers wanted to see them regardless. "I thought we could use this to study the anatomy of a hoax," Meldrum says. Instead Meldrum's visit to a ridge in the Blue Mountains set him firmly on a quest he has been on since.

Meldrum, an associate professor of anatomy and anthropology at Idaho State University, is an expert on foot morphology and locomotion in monkeys, apes, and hominids. He has studied the evolution of bipedalism and edited *From Biped to Strider* (Springer, 2004), a well-respected textbook. He brought his anatomical expertise to the site outside Walla Walla. The 14-inch-long prints Freeman showed him were interesting, Meldrum says, because some turned out at a 45-degree angle, suggesting that whatever made them had looked back over its shoulder. Some showed skin whorls, some were flat with distinct anatomical detail, others were of running feet–imprints of the front part of the foot only, of toes gripping the mud. Meldrum made casts and decided it would be hard to hoax the running footprints, "unless you had some device, some cable-loaded flexible toes."

To Meldrum, the anatomy captured in those prints and the casts of others he has examined as well as still unidentified hairs, recordings of strange calls and certain witness testimonials all add up to valid evidence that warrants study. He reviews that evidence in *Sasquatch: Legend Meets Science* (Forge, 2006). "My book is not an attempt to convince people of the existence of Sasquatch," the 49-year-old Meldrum says emphatically; rather it argues that "the evidence that exists fully justifies the investigation and the pursuit of this question."

To Meldrum's critics–including university colleagues and scientists in his own field–that same collection does not constitute valid evidence, and Meldrum's examination of it is pseudoscientific: belief shrouded in the language of scientific rigor and analysis. "Even if you have a million pieces of evidence, if all the evidence is inconclusive, you can't count it all up to make something conclusive," says David J. Daegling, an anthropologist at the University of Florida who has critiqued Meldrum and the Bigfoot quest in the *Skeptical Inquirer* and is the author of *Bigfoot Exposed* (AltaMira, 2004).

Neither side can win its case without a Sasquatch specimen or fossil or without the true confessions of a fleet of perhaps fleet-footed hoaxers. In the meantime, observers watch a debate that is striking in that both sides use virtually the same language, refute each other's interpretations with the same tone of disbelief, and insist they have the identical goal: honoring the scientific method. And the question of how science on the fringe should be dealt with remains open: some observers say that Meldrum, who has been lambasted by colleagues and passed over for promotion twice, should just be left alone to do his thing; others counter that in this era of creationism, global warming denial, and widespread antiscience sentiment and scientific illiteracy, it is particularly imperative that bad science be soundly scrutinized and exposed.

Meldrum is a tall, mustached man, relaxed, friendly, and gregarious. On a recent summer morning in his office–rich in Bigfoot paraphernalia–he explains that his interest in the subject arose when he was 11 and saw Roger Patterson's now famous film of an alleged Sasquatch loping into the forest. Meldrum listed cryptozoology (the study of hidden creatures such as yeti and Nessie) as an interest on his vitae when he applied for doctoral work. But Bigfoot as an active pursuit did not emerge until he arrived at Idaho State in 1993 and was back in the Pacific Northwest, where he grew up.

Meldrum's laboratory houses more than 200 casts relating to Bigfoot. As he pulls out drawers and talks about the casts, Meldrum shows ones with the hallmarks of hoax and others that intrigue him because of anatomy, hair striations, musculature, and an apparent midtarsal break–a pair of joints in the middle of the ape foot that have less mobility in the human foot because of the arch. He brings out a particularly controversial piece called the Skookum cast that he thinks may be of a reclining Sasquatch and others think may be of a reclining elk. "There is a chance we are wrong," he says. "But with the footprints, I feel more certain." Discounting the unusual casts "isn't scientific in the least," Meldrum maintains, and "it is irresponsible."

"He does bring more scientific rigor to this question than anyone else in the past, and he does do state-of-the-art footprint analysis," notes David R. Begun, a paleoanthropologist at the University of Toronto. Todd R. Disotell, a New York University anthropologist, agrees: "He is trying to bring rigor to it." Both researchers collaborate with Meldrum even though they do not accept his hypothesis that a large apelike creature exists. "If he hands me a feces sample or a bloodstain or a hair shaft, I am willing to do what I do with anything I get," Disotell says. "I go along with this because I am either doing good science, finding alternatives or debunking, or I have the find of the century." Disotell gets Bigfoot jibes over beers sometimes, but nothing similar to what Meldrum experiences: "I think what is happening to him is a shame."

In his famous "Cargo Cult Science" lecture in 1974, Richard Feynman described scientific thinking and integrity as "a kind of utter honesty–a kind of leaning over backwards" to raise and examine every doubt, every interpretation. This kind of thinking, critics say, is missing from Meldrum's Bigfoot work, whereas it infuses his fossil and primate gait research. Meldrum's principal critic from his own field is Daegling, who concludes that the "evidence doesn't look better on deeper analysis, it looks worse." He adds that "this isn't about Bigfoot–it is about how scientists go about doing their work and how we should be self-reflective and self-critical."

Meldrum responds by saying that most people do not see him critically sifting through all the evidence that comes his way–and discarding most of it. But if he is at times frustrated and beleaguered by skeptics, it appears some in his community are beleaguered by his exhortation that more researchers accept his interpretations or become involved. In reviewing Meldrum's and Daegling's books in the *American Journal of Physical Anthropology*, Matt Cartmill of Duke University concludes that if the chances of Bigfoot's being real are one in 10,000 (his admittedly wild guess), then having one physical anthropologist on the case seems a reasonable allocation of professional resources and that Meldrum does not deserve scorn or abuse. But Cartmill, who notes that he is "mortally certain" there is no Sasquatch, is irked by Meldrum's trying to guilt-trip those who do not do Bigfoot work and his disparaging them as lazy or aloof.

The tension is inevitable for science on the fringe, says Trent D. Stephens of Idaho State, who co-authored a book with Meldrum on evolutionary biology and Mormonism. As he puts it: "The stuff that is on the margins, the stuff that isn't popular–we scientists are horrible at judging it. And we say our mistakes about the fringe are all historical; we claim we are not making those mistakes today."

About the Author

Marguerite Holloway is a contributing editor for Scientific American.

A True and Complete Account of the Neuroscience of Zombies

By Gareth Cook

The wait has been long, but the discipline of neuroscience has finally delivered a full-length treatment of the zombie phenomenon. In their book, *Do Zombies Dream of Undead Sheep?*, scientists Timothy Verstynen and Bradley Voytek cover just about everything you might want to know about the brains of the undead. And if you learn some serious neuroscience along the way, well, that's fine with them too. Voytek answered questions from Mind Matters editor Gareth Cook.

Q: How is it that you and your coauthor came to write a book about zombies? Clearly it is an urgent public health threat, but I would not have expected a book from neuroscientists on the topic.

A: Indeed! You think you're prepared for the zombie apocalypse and then–BAM!–it happens, and only then do you realize how poorly prepared you really were. Truly the global concern of our time. (Obviously the zombie apocalypse won't actually happen, but hey, if it gets people thinking about emergency preparedness, then that's a good thing. Good enough for the CDC, apparently.)

Anyway, this whole silly thing started when Tim and I would get together to watch zombie movies with our wives and friends. Turns out when you get some neuroscientists together to watch zombie movies, after a few beers they start to diagnose them and mentally dissect their brains. Back in the summer of 2010, zombie author and enthusiast–and head of the Zombie Research Society–Matt Mogk got in touch with me to see if we were interested in doing something at the intersection of zombies and neuroscience. Given that Tim and I had already chatted about this in the past, we decided to take him up on it.

Honestly this whole thing is a trick. A cheat. It's our underhanded way of getting people to learn something about real neuroscience, but we've dressed it up in gross, decaying, undead clothing. Neuroscience has a broad popular appeal, but it's easy to misrepresent and/or overhype relatively mundane findings. Neuroscience is also incredibly complex, which makes it hard to accurately communicate to the non-scientific lay public the reality of the field. So we use zombies as a hook.

Less scrupulous people use neuroscience to peddle their serious BS; we're using BS to peddle serious neuroscience.

I much prefer the latter.

Q: What are some of the things you are able to explain, with the help of zombies?

A: We start with the obvious stuff: why do zombies move with such a slow, unsteady gait? Why can't they talk? Do they feel pain? We use those obvious questions as stepping stones toward what we hope is a much more nuanced view of the modern neuroscientific understanding of how the three or so pounds of brain in your head can give rise to the complexities of the human experience.

Each chapter tackles a specific behavioral trait relevant to zombies, including movement, hunger, emotions, speech, and cognition. Quite frankly, we go into excruciating neuroscientific detail, but we pepper each chapter with (sometimes very strange!) anecdotes from the history of brain research.

We wrote the book with the intent that it could serve as an introductory neuroscience text.

Q: Can you please explain the title, *Do Zombies Dream of Undead Sheep?*

A: It's an homage to Philip K. Dick's beautiful book, *Do Androids Dream of Electric Sheep*, which was later adapted by Ridley Scott into the movie *Bladerunner*, with a phenomenal performance by Harrison Ford as Rick Deckard.

The story is complex, but in part it is about what it means to be human. Hence the book's title, which is an allusion to the question of consciousness in artificial intelligence. In our book we touch a bit on the question of whether zombies are conscious–whether they have that spark of self-awareness we associate with being human. This is a deep question–perhaps *the* question–in the philosophy of mind.

It's also a play, because in the philosophy of mind, there is a thought experiment that asks the reader to imagine a person, exactly like you or I or any other person in every conceivable way, except for the fact that they lack self-awareness/consciousness/sentience. This imaginary being is referred to as a "philosophical zombie," or a "p-zombie."

Q: What is the strongest case for zombie consciousness? And the case against?

A: The strongest case for comes from the recent movie *Warm Bodies* wherein some of the less desiccated zombies, such as the protagonist R, have a rich internal dialogue, self-awareness, and emotions (though they can't always exert control over their behaviors). Similarly, the alternative universe run of the Marvel Zombies comics also shows the zombie superheroes and villains as being capable of complex thoughts and behaviors indicative of consciousness. But these are pretty rare examples, as the vast majority of zombie movies show them as mindless killers.

So I guess the strongest case against zombie consciousness would pretty much be the entirety of the zombie genre. Granted, it's quite difficult to define consciousness, but much like U.S. Supreme Court Justice Potter Stewart's views on pornography, most of us, "know it when we see it," and zombies ain't it.

Q: Can you tell me what you learned about Haitian zombies?

A: I learned that belief can be a very powerful thing. Well, belief combined with very powerful neurotoxins and hallucinogens, anyway.

We go into detail in our book about the cultural roots of the Haitian zombie. The word "zombie" comes from an African root word "nzambi," meaning "spirit of a dead person." Within Vodou, a priest (bokor) can sometimes be asked to take possession of the soul of a particularly troubled or threatening individual. The bokor induces "death" and separates the "little good angel" spirit (the ti bon ange) from the body. Once "resurrected," the physical body of the person is then forced to work at the will of the bokor.

An anthropological investigation by the ethnobotanist Wade Davis postulated that the process of making a Haitian zombi is neuropharmacological, wherein bokor use a chemical found in many animals (especially puffer fish), called tetrodotoxin (TTX), to paralyze their targets and induce a near death-like state in them. A sublethal dose of TTX allows the person to "die" and be "resurrected." During the recovery, the victim is forced to consume datura, a plant that contains chemicals such as scopolamine and hyoscyamine, powerful hallucinogens that leave the person delirious and compliant. Datura leaves the victim in an altered state of mind that makes them easily coercible.

The whole idea is fascinating. It sounds so far-fetched and unbelievable, but from a neuroscientific and psychological perspective, it's not impossible.

Can You Escape Zombies If You Smell Like Death?

By Josh Fischman

The apocalypse is nigh–or it certainly seems that way. We live besieged by deadly viruses, terrorist threats, and dunderheaded politicians. But what about zombies? Flesh-eating hordes of the walking dead, ever-growing, ever hungry, chasing us down alleys and forcing us to hide in dark basements.

Not, however, if chemist Raychelle Burks can help us with her "death cologne" camouflage method. Burks is a postdoctoral research fellow at Doane College in Nebraska and the University of Nebraska–Lincoln, where she studies new materials for sensors. And as a sensor expert and zombie aficionado–she has published on the topic, with scientific references–she believes we can fool zombies by smelling just like them. Burks told *Scientific American* that she has already identified the chemicals we need.

[An edited transcript of the interview follows.]

Q: How do you know zombies track you by smell?

A: Drawing on our bank of knowledge about zombies, which comes from pop culture, one thing that is constant is that zombies are brainless. They are awkward, they moan instead of talking, they repeatedly do stupid things. They have serious neurological deficiencies. Yet they try and eat us and not each other. How do they know we are not zombies? Well, you don't smell right. You smell alive, not dead and decomposing.

Q: What does dead and decomposing smell like?

A: There has been a lot of research in the nonfictional world about this. Scientists have helped crime scene investigators who look for hidden graves and trainers of dogs that search for human remains, and they have identified hundreds of compounds that come from rotting corpses. I've smelled several of them personally and, well, eeewwww.

Q: What are some of these odorous chemicals?

A: Putrescine and cadaverine are two that are appropriately named. They form when amino acids break down and they smell kind of skunky, and sulfurous, and like human feces. Then there is dimethyl disulfide, which smells like rotting cabbage. A related compound, dimethyl trisulfide, smells like an open, festering wound. Another chemical produced by rotting flesh, skatole, also makes people think of feces when they get a whiff.

Q: Lovely. How can all this help us with zombies?

A: We want to disguise ourselves, blend in with the surroundings, like hunters who spray themselves with animal urine. Our surroundings, however, are the walking dead. We need to cover up our natural scent to fool this environment. We need to smell like zombies. There has been a successful clinical trial of this approach: In the first season of the TV show *The Walking Dead* the people covered themselves with zombie goo to escape. Fortunately, chemistry provides an easier solution.

Q: That would be your "death cologne"?

A: Or "Eau de Death," yes. We would want to bring in marketing people before we settle on a name. But the idea is to create something out of these chemicals that you could spray on, instead of trying to smear yourself with zombie guts.

Q: Have you made the cologne yet?

A: Not yet. We'd need to bring in some cosmetic chemists, people who work on perfumes, to figure out how to bind these chemicals so they would last for a while. Should it be oil-based? A lotion, maybe a spray? You'd probably want lots of options—maybe a cream for personal use and a spray to camouflage where you live, so your house would not smell so alive. Then we would test it with human-remains dogs. We do not want to be testing in the middle of a zombie apocalypse. We want to know we have something that works.

Q: You really think this would work?

A: There are examples of it in nature. The corpse flower, for one. It has this giant bloom that smells like rot. The smell attracts insects that usually go for carrion, like flies and beetles, and the flower uses them to help spread its pollen. I've stood next to a blooming corpse flower and really, whew! I feel assured we are on the right track.

Q: So a plague of zombies does not scare you?

A: This Halloween I'm more worried about being hurt by a cow. I live in Nebraska. Statistically, the probability is much higher.

About the Author

Josh Fischman is a senior editor at Scientific American *who covers medicine, biology, and science policy. He has written and edited about science and health for* Discover, Science, Earth, *and* U.S. News & World Report.

Avoiding Zombie Attacks with Social Psychology

By Melanie Tannenbaum

The time has come. It's the zombie apocalypse.

You're approaching a zombie hoard with a group of several other brain-intact companions, and you need to figure out the best way to run past them. Where should you turn?

First, perhaps you should turn to social psychology.

There is an infamous parable, a now-classic staple in psychology classrooms across the country, about Kitty Genovese—the woman who was supposedly murdered in Queens in front of dozens of onlookers who failed to do anything to help, each person assuming that the other bystanders would assume responsibility.[1] This phenomenon is known as *diffusion of responsibility* or the *bystander effect*. Essentially, the larger any group gets, the less likely it is that any single person in that group will intervene or take action when confronted with any given situation, because each individual sees more other people around who could take responsibility or "pick up the slack," so to say.

Most of the time, when we talk about the bystander effect, we focus on its negative effects and implications, emphasizing the undesirability by providing suggestions for how to reverse it and how to get help from a crowd when you need it. But, instead of focusing on those aspects, I'm going to take a slightly less common approach. I'm going to discuss one way that you could potentially use your knowledge of the bystander effect to your (safe and legal) advantage.

The hypothesis I'm presenting here was first tested three years ago at the Run For Your Lives Zombie 5K, where I (and a few thousand others) attempted to complete a 5K course filled with volunteers who were dressed up like zombies and trying to steal our "lives" (aka flags on a belt around our waists). Sure enough, most of the runners attempted an obvious strategy: Attempting to run *around* the zombies, skirting off to the edge of the path and trying to dodge them as quickly as possible. The problem with this approach, however, is that the zombie closest to the edge clearly recognizes that it is his or her responsibility to take you down.

Instead, using my knowledge of social psychology, I tried a different, seemingly stupid tactic: *Running directly through the middle of the pack*. Sure enough, every time I tried to run around the pack, the zombie on the end reached out and grabbed one of my flags...but every time I sprinted straight through the middle of a giant pack of zombies, even though you would logically think that this would be the quickest way to lose your flags, the zombies all stood there and simply watched me run by, expecting one of the others to be the one to "take me down."

Lo and behold, I was able to make it through alive with one of my flags still intact, mostly thanks to my social psychology know-how (and a good amount of sprinting, to be fair).

So, if push comes to shove and it's time for the zombie apocalypse[2] (or if you simply find yourself wanting to compete in a Zombie 5K), use social psychology to your advantage: Run straight through the pack, instead of trying to dodge around it. Diffusion of responsibility can work to your advantage if you need to survive this spooky-scary weekend. And hey, if the zombies are coming after you for your tasty, super-smart, ultra-cunning braaaaaaaaaiiiiiiiins, it only seems fair to turn the tables on them by manipulating theirs instead.

Referenced

1. Although this story is a staple in Intro Social Psych classrooms around the country, more recent evidence has suggested that the "Kitty Genovese Case" may not have gone down exactly as it has been legacized. However, even those involved in debunking parts of the Kitty Genovese case have steadfastly claimed that the "bystander effect" is real and dangerous, and specific details about the Genovese case should not undermine this fact.
2. Yes, although Zombie 5Ks consist of living people with human reasoning capabilities, actual zombies would probably not follow the "rules" of human psychology. Let's just go with it.

About the Author

Melanie Tannenbaum is a freelance writer and science communications consultant currently living in the Bay Area. She received her Ph.D. in social psychology from the University of Illinois at Urbana-Champaign in 2015, where her research focused on the science of persuasion and motivation regarding political, environmental, and health-related behavior.

Bugs in the Brain

By Robert Sapolsky

Like most scientists, I attend professional meetings every now and then, one of them being the annual meeting of the Society for Neuroscience, an organization of most of the earth's brain researchers. This is one of the more intellectually assaulting experiences you can imagine. About 28,000 of us science nerds jam into a single convention center. After a while, this togetherness can make you feel pretty nutty: for an entire week, go into any restaurant, elevator, or bathroom, and the folks standing next to you will be having some animated discussion about squid axons. The process of finding out about the science itself is no easier. The meeting has 14,000 lectures and posters, a completely overwhelming amount of information. Of the subset of those posters that are essential for you to check, a bunch remain inaccessible because of the enthusiastic crowds in front of them, one turns out to be in a language you don't even recognize, and another inevitably reports every experiment you planned to do for the next five years. Amid it all lurks the shared realization that despite zillions of us slaving away at the subject, we still know squat about how the brain works.

My own low point at the conference came one afternoon as I sat on the steps of the convention center, bludgeoned by information and a general sense of ignorance. My eyes focused on a stagnant, murky puddle of water by the curb, and I realized that some microscopic bug festering in there probably knew more about the brain than all of us neuroscientists combined.

My demoralized insight stemmed from a paper about how certain parasites control the brain of their host. Most of us know that bacteria, protozoa, and viruses have astonishingly sophisticated ways of using animal bodies for their own purposes. They hijack our cells, our energy, and our lifestyles so they can thrive. But in many ways, the most dazzling and fiendish thing that such parasites have evolved—and the subject that occupied my musings that day—is their ability to change a host's behavior for their own ends. Some textbook examples involve ectoparasites, organisms that colonize the surface of the body. For instance, certain mites of the genus *Antennophorus* ride on the backs of ants and, by stroking an ant's mouthparts, can trigger a reflex that culminates in the ant's disgorging food for the mite to feed on. A species of pinworm of the genus *Syphacia* lays eggs on a rodent's skin, the eggs secrete a substance that causes itchiness, the rodent grooms the itchy spot with its teeth, the eggs get ingested in the process, and once inside the rodent they happily hatch.

These behavioral changes are essentially brought about by annoying a host into acting in a way beneficial to the interlopers. But some parasites actually alter the function of the nervous system itself. Sometimes they achieve this change indirectly, by manipulating hormones that affect the nervous system. There are barnacles (*Sacculina granifera*), a form of crustacean, found in Australia that attach to male sand crabs and secrete a feminizing hormone that induces maternal behavior. The zombified crabs then migrate out to sea with brooding females and make depressions in the sand ideal for dispersing larvae. The males, naturally, won't be releasing any. But the barnacles will. And if a barnacle infects a female crab, it induces the same behavior—after atrophying the female's ovaries, a practice called parasitic castration.

Bizarre as these cases are, at least the organisms stay outside the brain. Yet a few do manage to get inside. These are microscopic ones, mostly viruses rather than relatively gargantuan creatures like mites, pinworms, and barnacles. Once one of these tiny parasites is inside the brain, it remains fairly sheltered from immune attack, and it can go to work diverting neural machinery to its own advantage.

The rabies virus is one such parasite. Although the actions of this virus have been recognized for centuries, no one I know of has framed them in the neurobiological manner I'm about to. There are lots of ways rabies could have evolved to move between hosts. The virus didn't have to go anywhere near the brain. It could have devised a trick similar to the one employed by the agents that cause nose colds—namely, to irritate nasal-passage nerve endings, causing the host to sneeze and spritz viral replicates all over, say, the person sitting in front of him or her at the movies. Or the virus could have induced an insatiable desire to lick someone or some animal, thereby passing on virus shed into the saliva. Instead, as we all know, rabies can cause its host to become aggressive so the virus can jump into another host via saliva that gets into the wounds.

Just think about this. Scads of neurobiologists study the neural basis of aggression: the pathways of the brain that are involved, the relevant neurotransmitters, the interactions between genes and environment, modulation by hormones, and so on. Aggression has spawned conferences, doctoral theses, petty academic squabbles, nasty tenure disputes, the works. Yet all along, the rabies virus has "known" just which neurons to infect to make a victim rabid. And as far as I am aware, no neuroscientist has studied rabies specifically to understand the neurobiology of aggression.

Despite how impressive these viral effects are, there is still room for improvement. That is because of the parasite's nonspecificity. If you are a rabid animal, you might bite one of the few creatures that rabies does not replicate well in, such as a rabbit. So although the behavioral effects of infecting the brain are quite dazzling, if the parasite's impact is too broad, it can wind up in a dead-end host.

Which brings us to a beautifully specific case of brain control and the paper I mentioned earlier, by Manuel Berdoy and his colleagues at the University of Oxford. Berdoy and his associates study a parasite called *Toxoplasma gondii*. In a toxoplasmic utopia, life consists of a two-host sequence involving rodents and cats. The protozoan gets ingested by a rodent, in which it forms cysts throughout the body, particularly in the brain. The rodent gets eaten by a cat, in which the *toxoplasma* organism reproduces. The cat sheds the parasite in its feces, which, in one of those circles of life, is nibbled by rodents. The whole scenario hinges on specificity: cats are the only species in which *toxoplasma* can sexually reproduce and be shed. Thus, *toxoplasma* wouldn't want its carrier rodent to get picked off by a hawk or its cat feces ingested by a dung beetle. Mind you, the parasite can infect all sorts of other species; it simply has to wind up in a cat if it wants to spread to a new host.

This potential to infect other species is the reason all those "what to do during pregnancy" books recommend banning the cat and its litter box from the house and warn pregnant women against gardening if there are cats wandering about. If *toxoplasma* from cat feces gets into a pregnant woman, it can get into the fetus, potentially causing neurological damage. Well-informed pregnant women get skittish around cats. *Toxoplasma*-infected rodents, however, have the opposite reaction. The parasite's extraordinary trick has been to make rodents lose their skittishness.

All good rodents avoid cats—a behavior ethologists call a fixed-action pattern, in that the rodent doesn't develop the aversion because of trial and error (since there aren't likely to be many opportunities to learn from one's errors around cats). Instead feline phobia is hardwired. And it is accomplished through olfaction in the form of pheromones, the chemical odorant signals that animals release. Rodents instinctually shy away from the smell of a cat—even rodents that have never seen a cat in their lives, rodents that are the descendants of hundreds of generations of lab animals. Except for those infected with *toxoplasma*. As Berdoy and his group have shown, those rodents selectively lose their aversion to, and fear of, cat pheromones.

Now, this is not some generic case of a parasite messing with the head of the intermediate host and making it scatterbrained and vulnerable. Everything else seems pretty intact in the rodents. The social status of the animal doesn't change in its dominance hierarchy. It is still interested in mating and thus, de facto, in the pheromones of the opposite sex. The infected rodents can still distinguish other odors. They simply don't recoil from cat pheromones. This is flabbergasting. This is akin to someone getting infected with a brain parasite that has no effect whatsoever on the person's thoughts, emotions, SAT scores, or television preferences but, to complete its life cycle, generates an irresistible urge to go to the zoo, scale a fence, and try to French-kiss the pissiest-looking polar bear. A parasite-induced fatal attraction, as Berdoy's team noted in the title of its paper.

Obviously, more research is needed. I say this not only because it is obligatory at this point in any article about science, but because this finding is just so intrinsically cool that someone has to figure out how it works. And because–permit me a Stephen Jay Gould moment–it provides ever more evidence that evolution is amazing. Amazing in ways that are counterintuitive. Many of us hold the deeply entrenched idea that evolution is directional and progressive: invertebrates are more primitive than vertebrates, mammals are the most evolved of vertebrates, primates are the genetically fanciest mammals, and so forth. Some of my best students consistently fall for that one, no matter how much I drone on in lectures. If you buy into that idea big-time, you're not just wrong, you're not all that many steps away from a philosophy that has humans directionally evolved as well, with the most evolved being northern Europeans with a taste for schnitzel and goose-stepping.

So remember, creatures are out there that can control brains. Microscopic and even larger organisms that have more power than Big Brother and, yes, even neuroscientists. My reflection on a curbside puddle brought me to the opposite conclusion that Narcissus reached in his watery reflection. We need phylogenetic humility. We are certainly not the most evolved species around, nor the least vulnerable. Nor the cleverest.

About the Author

Robert M. Sapolsky is a professor of biological sciences, neurology, and neurological sciences at Stanford University and a research associate at the National Museums of Kenya. In his laboratory work, he focuses on how stress can damage the brain and on gene therapy for the nervous system. He also studies populations of wild baboons in East Africa, trying to determine the relation between the social rank of a baboon and its health.

Protozoa Could Be Controlling Your Brain

By Christof Koch

The ancient debate surrounding the existence of free will appears unresolvable, a metaphysical question that generates much heat yet little light. Common sense and volumes of psychological and neuroscientific research reveal, however, that we are less free than we think we are. Our genes, our upbringing, and our environment influence our behaviors in ways that often escape conscious control. Understanding this influence, the advertisement industry spent approximately half a trillion dollars worldwide in 2010 to shape the buying decisions of consumers. And extreme dictatorships, such as that in North Korea, remain in power through the effective use of insidious and all-pervasive forms of propaganda. Yet nothing approaches the perfidy of the one-celled organism *Toxoplasma gondii*, one of the most widespread of all parasitic protozoa. It takes over the brain of its host and makes it do things, even actions that will cause it to die, in the service of this nasty hitchhiker. It sounds like a cheesy Hollywood horror flick, except that it is for real.

We know that illness in general can slow us down, incapacitate us and, in the worst case, kill us. Yet this organism is much more specific. Natural selection has given rise to pathogens that infiltrate the nervous system and change that system's wiring to achieve its ultimate purpose, replication–like a computer virus that reprograms an infected machine.

Such is the case with *T. gondii*. It sexually reproduces only in the intestines of cats yet can maintain itself indefinitely in any warm-blooded animal. Infected cats shed millions of their oocysts in their feces. Taken up by all kinds of animals, including dogs, rodents and humans, they infect muscle and the brain to escape attacks by the host's immune system. Hidden away, they remain dormant as cysts, surrounding themselves with a tough cell wall. Yet this quiet stage of infection, called toxoplasmosis, is deceptive. Violating all rules of good hospitality, these invaders make the host's brain do things counterproductive to its own survival.

Toxoplasmosis has been most thoroughly studied in rats and mice. Both species have a deep-seated, innate fear of cats for obvious reasons. Spray a bit of cat urine into a corner, and the rodent will avoid this location, well, like the plague. In contrast, an infected animal loses its innate fear of cats. By some measures, it even appears to be mildly attracted to the smell of felines. This is an unfortunate turn of events for the rodent, because it is now more likely to be successfully hunted by a cat. On the other hand, this is a great deal for *T. gondii*. When the cat devours the sick critter and its contaminated brain, *T. gondii* moves into its final host, where it reproduces, completing its life cycle. Not quite what the romantics have in mind when they write about "the circle of life"!

The behavioral manipulation induced by *T. gondii* is quite specific. The infected rodent doesn't look sick; its weight is normal; it moves about normally, possibly a bit more frantically than other mice; it grooms itself; and it interacts routinely with its conspecifics. Think how different this case is from what happens in rabies, another nasty infection. The animal loses its instinctual shyness, aggressively attacking others (the proverbial mad dog), thereby spreading the rabies virus through its bite. But because *T. gondii* can reproduce only in felines, it wants its host to be eaten by cats, not by just any carnivore. And because cats hunt live prey and do not eat carrion, *T. gondii* must not immediately kill its temporary host.

Rodents Aren't Superheroes

How does *T. gondii* effect its insidious changes in the host? Experiments by Joanne P. Webster of Imperial College London, Robert Sapolsky of Stanford University, and others have shown that infected rats or mice do not turn into the murine equivalent of Siegfried, the hero of Wagner's *Ring* who knew no fear. No, they still avoid open spaces, remain nocturnal creatures, retain their aversion to the urine of other predators, and learn to fear a tone associated with a foot shock. Might the protozoa have stunted their smell? After all, if they cannot smell anything anymore, they would not know how to avoid places smelling of cat urine. But infected mice still avoid food if it smells different–an aversion that arose partly because for centuries humans have been trying to control rodents by poison. The infected mice also respond appropriately to the smell of their littermates.

Clues about how the parasites affect the animal come from several observations. First, the density of cysts in the amygdala is almost double that in other brain structures involved in odor perception. Parts of the amygdala have been linked to anxiety and the sensation of fear. Second, the genome of *T. gondii* contains two genes related to mammalian genes involved in the regulation of dopamine, the molecule associated with reward and pleasure signals in the brain, including in ours. So perhaps the creepy protozoa makes suicidal activities, such as hanging around places frequented by cats, feel more pleasurable for the infected rodent?

What elevates this vignette about evolution and life in the wild to epic proportions for humanity is that about a tenth of the U.S. population is infected by *T. gondii* (in some countries, such as France, the infection rate is seven to eight times higher, possibly because of the widespread consumption of uncooked and undercooked meat). Human toxoplasmosis is usually considered to be symptom-free (what doctors refer to as asymptomatic). Exceptions are patients with a weakened immune system and the unborn (hence the need for pregnant women to avoid cleaning cat-litter boxes).

Science has known for a long time that schizophrenic patients are two to three times more likely to carry antibodies to *T. gondii* than are controls who are not schizophrenic. Furthermore, antipsychotic drugs that block the action of dopamine, such as haloperidol, commonly used in the treatment of schizophrenia, are also effective in combating toxoplasmosis in both rats and people. And some infected adults go on to develop psychotic symptoms similar to schizophrenia. Little is known about the mode or site of action of this pathogen in the human brain. The exact link between *T. gondii* and psychiatric diseases is tantalizing but remains murky.

Recent claims go so far as to argue for a role of *T. gondii* in shaping distinct cultural habits, depending on the rate of infection in the population. A prospective study tracking the road safety in Czech recruits during their 18 months of compulsory military draft found a rate of accidents six times higher in affected drivers. Are the young men with toxoplasmosis infection simply slowed down? Or do they drive more aggressively?

In my November 2009 column, I described the discovery by cognitive neuroscientists that the feeling of freely willing an action (called authorship or agency) is a subjective, conscious sensation no different, in principle, from the conscious awareness of seeing the azure blue sky or feeling the sharp pain of a toothache. When I engage in a dangerous pursuit, such as taking the end of the rope on a steep section of a granite wall in Yosemite Valley while climbing, I feel as if "I freely decided" to do so, whatever this might mean in a metaphysical sense. Yet my action is most likely caused by an inexhaustible multiplicity of factors not accessible to my conscious introspection, including, yes, possibly some tiny single-celled parasites lodging in my brain and making me act out their silent commands. The wonder of it all.

About the Author

Christof Kock is Lois and Victor Troendle Professor of Cognitive and Behavioral Biology at the California Institute of Technology. He serves on Scientific American Mind*'s board of advisers.*

Played by a Parasite

By Gustavo Arrizabalaga and Bill Sullivan

Imagine a world without fear. It might be empowering to go about your daily life uninhibited by everyday distresses. You could cross highways with confidence, take on all kinds of daredevilry, and watch horror flicks without flinching. Yet consider the prospect a little more deeply, and the possibilities become darker, even deadly. Our fears, after all, can protect us.

The basic aversion that a mouse has for a cat, for instance, keeps the rodent out of death's jaws. But unfortunately for mice everywhere, there is a second enemy with which to contend, one that may prevent them from experiencing that fear in the first place. A unicellular organism (a protozoan), *Toxoplasma gondii*, can override a rodent's most basic survival instincts. The result is a rodent that does not race away from a cat but is instead strangely attracted to it.

Toxoplasma's reach extends far beyond the world of cat and mouse. It may have a special relationship with rodent and feline hosts, but this parasite also infects the brains of billions of animals on land, at sea, and in the air. Humans are no exception. Worldwide, scientists estimate that as many as three billion people may be carrying *Toxoplasma*. In the U.S., there is a one-in-five chance that *Toxoplasma* parasites are lodged in your neural circuits, and infection rates are as high as 95 percent in other countries.

For most people, this infection appears asymptomatic, but recent evidence shows that *Toxoplasma* actively remodels the molecular landscape of mammalian brain cells. Now some researchers have begun to speculate that this tiny single-celled organism may be tweaking human health and personalities in stealthy, subtle ways.

What the Cat Dragged In

Researchers first discovered *T. gondii* in 1908, and by the end of the 20th century they had a good grasp on how people could pick up this parasite. The story starts with cats: for reasons that scientists have yet to unravel, *Toxoplasma* can sexually reproduce only in the feline gut. The parasite breeds within its feline host and is released from the feline's tail end. Cats are such obsessive groomers that it is rarely found in their fur. Instead people can become infected from kitty litter or by ingesting it in contaminated water or food.

Within a new host the parasite begins dividing asexually and spreading throughout the host's body. During this initial stage of the infection, *Toxoplasma* can cause the disease toxoplasmosis in immunocompromised or otherwise susceptible hosts, leading to extensive tissue damage. Pregnant women are particularly at risk. If a woman is infected with *Toxoplasma* for the first time during pregnancy, the parasite may invade the developing fetus, cutting through tissues and organs as it spreads from cell to cell. Infection early in pregnancy can result in miscarriage or birth defects.

In otherwise healthy individuals, however, the only symptoms during this period are brief, flulike discomforts such as chills, fever, and body ache. Within days the immune system gets the parasite under control, and *Toxoplasma* retreats into a dormant state. It conceals itself within a hardened wall in the host's cells, a structure called a tissue cyst.

This stage of the infection has no other discernible symptoms, but individuals with dormant infections who develop compromised immune systems–because of AIDS, an organ transplant, or chemotherapy–may experience severe complications. With the body's defense systems weakened, *Toxoplasma* can reactivate and grow uncontrollably.

Once infected, a person will remain a carrier for life. Our immune system is apparently incapable of eliminating the tissue cysts, nor can any known drug. Nevertheless, the infection, detectable with a blood test, has long been viewed as relatively benign. After all, many people carry this parasite with no obvious ill effects. Only recently have scientists begun reexamining this belief.

Eat Me, Mr. Kitty

In the 1980s researchers noticed unusual behaviors in *Toxoplasma*-infected mice. The rodents became hyperactive and groomed less. In 1994 epidemiologist Joanne Webster, then at the University of Oxford, observed that rats harboring tissue cysts behaved differently from their uninfected counterparts. Instead of fleeing from cats, the infected rodents moved toward them—making them easier prey.

Webster suspected that this "fatal feline attraction," as she called it, was a crafty way for the parasite to get back into a cat's belly to complete the sexual stage of its life cycle. In the years to follow, this idea gained ground: a large body of work now shows that the parasite can indeed manipulate rodents' behavior by altering neural activity and gene expression.

Several well-controlled experiments have shown that although uninfected rodents avoid areas that have been infused with cat stench, infected rodents do not seem to mind. Even more bizarre, in 2011 neuroendocrinologist Robert Sapolsky of Stanford University, molecular biologist Ajai Vyas of Nanyang Technological University in Singapore, and their colleagues found that—at least in terms of neural activity—infected rats appeared to be sexually attracted to cat scent.

In the mammalian brain, the "defensive" and "reproductive" neuronal pathways run in parallel. These pathways start at the olfactory bulb, involved in odor detection, and terminate at the limbic system, an area critical to basic reactions such as fear and arousal. Their proximity may partially explain how the parasite manipulates rodent behavior.

Working with 18 infected and 18 uninfected male rats, Sapolsky and his colleagues studied the rodents' behavior when they were exposed to either the odor of female rats or cat urine. Then they sacrificed the animals and looked at their brains. The researchers found a slight enrichment of parasite cysts in the limbic system compared with other brain areas.

They also assessed which parts of the brain had been operating during exposure to odors by staining the cells with a solution that revealed c-Fos, a protein expressed when neurons are active. The Stanford researchers discovered that infected rodents had high levels of engagement in their brain's reproductive pathway in response to the odor of both female rats and felines. In addition, the team found that infected rodents exposed to cat urine showed activation in the reproductive pathway similar to what uninfected rodents showed for the scent of a female rat. These results suggest that in infected rats, neural activity shifts from the defensive to the nearby reproductive pathway. Instead of smelling danger, the rats smell love.

Scientists are not sure how exactly the parasite elicits this fatal attraction, but one clue surfaced in 2014 in Vyas's laboratory. Vyas and his colleagues showed that *Toxoplasma* increases its host's levels of a neurotransmitter involved in social and sexual behavior. To accomplish this task, the parasite alters DNA methylation. Methylated genes are silent, blocked by a molecular cap. *Toxoplasma* uncaps a group of genes that spurs the creation of the sex-promoting neurotransmitter. Vyas and his team discovered this trick by performing the process in reverse: when they administered a chemical compound to the infected rats that silences the associated genes, the rats' peculiar attraction to feline odor vanished.

Kiss and Spit

With evidence mounting that *Toxoplasma* can influence its host's brain, other scientists set out to understand the parasite's effects at a much smaller scale: within each host cell. Their findings suggest that this microbe is particularly insidious–the changes it makes may be permanent.

To replicate, *Toxoplasma* must invade a cell. Stanford parasitologist John C. Boothroyd has dubbed this process "kiss and spit." The parasite first attaches to the host cell (the kiss) and then releases an arsenal of foreign proteins into that cell (the spit).

Toxoplasma then enters the host cell, and the injected proteins help it redecorate its new home.

The parasite's first act is establishing a protective bubble in which it can divide in peace without attacks from host cell proteins. (Later, during the infection's dormant stage, these bubbles thicken to become tissue cysts.) The parasite then moves the mitochondria, which serve as the cell's powerhouses, to be adjacent to the protective bubble. It also acts on the cell's DNA, inhibiting the expression of some host genes while activating others. Finally, *Toxoplasma* modifies host proteins to alter their function and inhibit the immune response.

Altogether, these modifications ensure that the host cell will live a long time and supply energy to the parasite, without alerting immune cells that a parasite has moved in. Although these findings have principally been made with rodents, work with human cell cultures suggests that the same changes probably take place in the human body. In our labs, we are studying how *Toxoplasma* replicates and interacts with its host in an effort to develop new drugs to treat this infection.

Remarkably, a study that Boothroyd's group published in 2012 showed that *Toxoplasma* not only spits into the cells it invades but also spits into cells that it does not infect. This behavior–spitting proteins in passing without lingering in the cells–is a recent discovery in the microbial world. Consequently, cells that are not harboring *Toxoplasma* contain parasite proteins that can co-opt and reprogram those cells. In the brains of infected mice, cells that have been spat into but not invaded are even more common than ones containing parasites. This widespread scattering of proteins means *Toxoplasma* can affect its host at a global level, making it easier to imagine how the parasite might manipulate the activity of an entire animal.

In 2013 biologist Michael Eisen of the University of California, Berkeley, and his colleagues found that a rodent's strange attraction to cat odors may be permanent, even if there are no longer signs of infection. In one study, Eisen exposed mice to a mutant strain of the parasite that does not appear to form brain cysts. Four months later the infected mice had no detectable parasites in the brain, yet they were still attracted to cat odors instead of repelled. This finding suggests that even if the parasite can be removed from the body, behavioral changes may persist. The infection leaves a mark, like a permanent parasite-given tattoo.

The Human Connection

The fact that people do not throw themselves into the lion cage at the zoo strongly argues that *Toxoplasma* does not affect humans in the way it transforms mice. Mammalian brains are not all the same, and *Toxoplasma*'s tricks are most likely specially suited for rodents. The parasite has little to gain, in evolutionary terms, by adapting to control the human brain. We are, after all, a "dead-end" host–the parasites within us are unlikely to return to the cat gut for breeding. Nevertheless, these cysts lodged in our brains could be manipulating us in subtle, unexpected ways. For example, a recent study by epidemiologist Angelico Mendy of the University of Iowa found a potential link between *Toxoplasma* infection in children and performance on cognitive exams. A large body of research, mostly conducted by parasitologist Jaroslav Flegr of Charles University in Prague, supports the idea that *Toxoplasma* harbors the potential to change human behavior. In a series of personality assessments spanning more than a decade and involving nearly 2,500 individuals, Flegr and his colleagues found that certain traits often coincide with a *Toxoplasma* infection. For example, infected men tend to be introverted, suspicious, and rebellious, whereas infected women tend to be extraverted, trusting, and obedient.

Using a simple reaction time test, Flegr has also found that infected individuals are slower to respond than uninfected peers. This lag may relate to another correlation he has identified. In a 2009 analysis of 3,890 military conscripts in the Czech Republic, those with latent toxoplasmosis who also had a negative blood type, meaning they lacked the protein RhD, were six times more likely to be in a fender bender than those who were *Toxoplasma*-free or who had a positive blood type. The function of RhD is unknown. Flegr's results suggest RhD somehow protects people against *Toxoplasma*'s effects, but how it does so remains a mystery.

More recently, Flegr and his colleagues found that some of the changes that occur in mice also exist in humans–albeit in a gender-specific manner. In 2011 the researchers asked 34 *Toxoplasma*-infected students and 134 noninfected students to rate the intensity and pleasantness of urine samples from different animals. Curiously, infected men found cat urine odor more pleasant than uninfected men; in women, the opposite occurred.

Another line of research has focused on a potential link between toxoplasmosis and schizophrenia. In 2001 psychiatrist E. Fuller Torrey of the Stanley Medical Research Institute and neurovirologist Robert Yolken of the Johns Hopkins University School of Medicine reported significantly more antibodies associated with *Toxoplasma* in patients experiencing their first schizophrenic episode as compared with healthy peers. Although this initial study was limited to only 38 people, additional studies in the ensuing years have largely supported this link.

Fascinating and attention-grabbing as these studies may be, they come with several caveats. The sample sizes are relatively small, meaning the findings are preliminary. They do not definitively demonstrate that *Toxoplasma* causes behavior changes in humans. In the case of schizophrenia, it is important to note that the condition is complex and may involve many triggers. The parasite may be one contributor, but it is also possible that people with schizophrenia may simply behave in ways that make them more likely to pick up an infection. No hard evidence has emerged to date that directly implicates the parasite as a cause for any psychosis, including schizophrenia.

Ultimately these provocative findings probably reflect a complex exchange among various factors. Certain genetic predispositions, for example, or even an interaction between *Toxoplasma* and another infectious agent could mean that some people are more susceptible to the parasite's persuasion. Only larger studies from multiple research groups will determine precisely what this parasite may do to the people it infects. Expanded studies might also help explain why *Toxoplasma* appears to have the opposite effects in men and women.

An Accidental Meddler

As researchers continue to uncover the astonishing effects that *Toxoplasma* has kept secret for so long, many scientists are beginning to think that *Toxoplasma*'s impressive cellular and molecular tricks make it capable of causing disruptions within a human host. At the very least, the findings from human surveys call for further clarification.

If you are curious whether you carry the parasite, you can get a blood test. In the meantime, you can increase your odds of staying *Toxoplasma*-free by maintaining good hygiene for you and your feline friends. If cats wander through your yard, the Centers for Disease Control and Prevention recommends wearing gloves and a mask when gardening and keeping any sandboxes closed up when not in use. Other basic health tips—cleaning fruits and vegetables, thoroughly cooking meats, and washing hands regularly—are also important for avoiding an infection.

The notion that *Toxoplasma* could radically reorient the brain and behavior is certainly disturbing. But perhaps these findings are a reminder of a more basic truth. Each person actually constitutes a rich ecosystem. For every human cell in the body, there are 10 more bacterial cells that influence physiology, metabolism, and health. The protozoan *Toxoplasma* is just another stowaway within the system and one that warrants more study. After all, we will never fully understand ourselves without learning about our microbial companions.

How *Toxoplasma* Conquered the Animal Kingdom

Toxoplasma gondii is the most widespread parasite on earth, found across all continents and in a staggering variety of habitats. We have only recently discovered how many different animals it infects. To the surprise of many, University of British Columbia scientists found the parasite in beluga whales in the Arctic in 2014. Off the California coast, *Toxoplasma* infection has been revealed to be responsible for sea otter deaths formerly attributed to sharks or boats.

The wily intruder owes its success in part to a high rate of expansion. A cat newly infected with *Toxoplasma* can excrete up to 800 million packets containing the parasite–called oocysts–in the span of about seven to 14 days. Once released, an oocyst can persist in soil or water for years. Inhaling or ingesting just one oocyst is enough to establish infection, which virtually guarantees that the parasite will find its way into a variety of new hosts.

But house cats may have unfairly gotten a bad reputation from their link to *Toxoplasma*. Pet owners may indeed accidentally ingest an oocyst if they fail to wash up after tending to kitty litter, but scientists believe an individual cat will shed oocysts only once in a lifetime.

In contrast to housebound felines, wild and feral cats can spread oocysts in gardens, farms, and water reservoirs, meaning they are likely to be greater contributors to *Toxoplasma*'s spread. Oocysts are commonly found in dirty water or on unwashed fruits and vegetables. The parasite does not infect plants, but its oocysts can remain on their surface unless they are carefully cleaned.

Moreover, many animals–including humans–are likely to become infected by eating raw or undercooked meat. Any animal infected by *Toxoplasma* will harbor tissue cysts for the rest of its life. When that tissue is eaten in, for instance, steak tartare, the parasite spreads into its new host. These clever methods of entering new hosts have allowed *Toxoplasma* to disseminate across the globe.

About the Authors

Gustavo Arrizabalaga and Bill Sullivan are professors of pharmacology and toxicology and of microbiology and immunology at the Indiana University School of Medicine. Each runs an independent research laboratory focused on the cellular and molecular biology of Toxoplasma gondii.

Microbes on Your Mind

By Moheb Costandi

The thought of parasites preying on your body or brain very likely sends shivers down your spine. Perhaps you imagine insectoid creatures bursting from stomachs or a malevolent force controlling your actions. These visions are not just the night terrors of science-fiction writers—the natural world is replete with such examples.

Take *Toxoplasma gondii*, the single-celled parasite. When mice are infected by it, they suffer the grave misfortune of becoming attracted to cats. Once a cat inevitably consumes the doomed creature, the parasite can complete its life cycle inside its new host. Or consider *Cordyceps*, the parasitic fungus that can grow into the brain of an insect. The fungus can force an ant to climb a plant before consuming its brain entirely. After the insect dies, a mushroom sprouts from its head, allowing the fungus to disperse its spores as widely as possible.

Microbes that manipulate the behavior of their host are not limited to nature's dark corners, although those examples are vivid. Our body hosts vast numbers of foreign microorganisms, some of which wield unseen powers over us. These microbes are not parasites—they live on and in our body, mostly in our gut, and often strike up a symbiotic relationship with us.

Composed mostly of bacteria but also viruses and fungi, this so-called gut microbiota churns out a complex cocktail of biologically active compounds. Some of these products closely resemble human hormones and neurotransmitters, the chemicals that neurons use to communicate with one another. Microbes in the gut (the small and large intestines and the stomach) have long been known to play a role in human health. Irritable bowel syndrome and stomach ulcers, for example, are linked to an imbalanced microbial population.

In the past few years scientists have been discovering that these microscopic inhabitants of our body may be subtly altering our moods, emotions, and perhaps even our personalities. Gut microbiota appear to alter gene activity in the brain and the development of key regions involved in memory and learning. These denizens of our intestines could help explain why psychiatric symptoms vary among individuals, as well as their responses to medications. Gut microbes could also account for some of the differences in mood, personality, and thought processes that occur within and among individuals.

Early clinical trials are even suggesting that probiotic supplements could treat mood disorders. Eventually we may learn that our bacterial soup contains markers for diseases, which could be detected cheaply and quickly. "Research into the gut microbiome has the potential to change many aspects of health and biotechnology," says molecular biophysicist Rob Knight of the University of Colorado at Boulder.

Your Microbial Self

From the minute you are born, microbes begin to colonize every exposed surface and organ of your body. By age three the gut contains a full complement of approximately 100 trillion microbes. According to most estimates, about 500 different bacterial species call your intestines home, with 30 to 40 species making up the bulk of the population. Family members' microbial compositions are more similar to one another than to unrelated people, and identical twins are most alike of all, suggesting that genetics helps to determine the intestinal inhabitants we acquire.

The variety among people can be glimpsed with something as simple as a swab of your computer keyboard. In 2010 Knight and his colleagues showed that the bacteria on a computer keyboard resembled the bacterial community on that computer user's fingers more closely than the populations dwelling on a different keyboard or another person's hand. The genomes of these microorganisms harbor approximately 100 times more genes than our own DNA. "Ninety percent of the cells in what we like to think of as 'our' bodies actually contain microbial genomes rather than human ones," he says.

The study of the gut's ecosystem is in its infancy, but interest in this area has been growing rapidly. Drastic reductions in the cost of DNA sequencing allow researchers to analyze large numbers of microbes simultaneously rather than having to grow them one at a time in the laboratory. Scientists can now quickly take a census of the gut and hunt for associations between microbiota and disease.

In 2007 the National Institutes of Health launched the Human Microbiome Project, a five-year, $115-million initiative to sequence the DNA of as many gut microbes as possible. The following year two more groups were created: the International Human Microbiome Consortium, which seeks to build a comprehensive database, and MetaHIT, an alliance of 13 partners drawn from eight European countries in academia and industry, with $43 million in funding. These projects all seek to understand how the species populating our gut relate to our health.

The composition of these communities is highly dynamic throughout life. Changes in diet, drugs, and other environmental factors can unleash earthquakes on our internal ecosystem. But freeloaders they are not. Bacteria help us digest food by fermenting dietary proteins and polysaccharides. They synthesize amino acids and minerals that the body needs but does not produce itself, and they protect us from pathogens by interacting with the immune system. Microbiome diversity appears to be a good indicator of general health–it decreases with age, and people with reduced diversity not only put on weight more easily than others but also struggle more to lose a few pounds. It should come as no surprise, then, that these microscopic creatures also meddle with the mind.

The Gut-Brain Connection

Anyone who has ever lost control of their bowels when scared is well aware of the intimate connection between the brain and the body's internal plumbing. We refer to "gut feelings" to describe an intuitive, emotional response, and we say that doing something daring "takes guts." Less obvious is that these responses are not merely emanating from a single lump of flesh, sophisticated as it may be.

Embedded in the lining of the intestines is the enteric nervous system, with hundreds of millions of neurons–one-thousandth the number in your brain. This network, colloquially termed a "second brain," controls gut function. It processes missives from the intestines and their microbes without input from brain number one. Gut neurons communicate with the brain through the vagus nerve, which extends from the base of the brain to the chest and abdomen and sends a branch of nerve fibers to the intestines.

The clearest connection between gut bacteria and the mind can be seen in how we experience anxiety and stress. In one influential study in 2004, for example, Nobuyuki Sudo of Kyushu University in Japan and his colleagues speculated that microbes might be involved in the brain's stress response. They had previously shown that gut microbes affect the development of the immune system early in life. The immune system, in turn, interacts extensively with the nervous system during this period. To investigate, they raised newborn mice in special conditions that prevented microbes from colonizing their guts. The rodents were then placed in situations designed to induce stress, in this case by restraining them.

Compared with normal mice, the germ-free mice had higher levels of stress hormones in their blood and reduced expression of the gene that codes for brain-derived neurotrophic factor (BDNF) in the hippocampus, a region important for memory formation and learning. When the brain generates new neurons, those young cells grow axons and dendrites that seek out networks of existing neurons to join. Those that encounter a burst of the protein BDNF during this process are more likely to survive and link up with other neurons; those that do not will wither away. Sudo's experiment suggested that gut microbes could influence the growth of memory and learning networks, which affected the rodents' ability to handle stress.

To strengthen the argument that microbes might be responsible for the changes, the researchers then colonized the germ-free mice with *Bifidobacterium infantis*, one of the most prevalent species in the microbiota and one of the first bacterial strains to settle into the gut of newborns, both human and rodent. The newly infected rodents' stress response quieted down to match that of the normal mice.

John Bienenstock and Jane Foster of the Brain-Body Institute at McMaster University in Ontario recently revisited this idea in a series of studies published in 2011. In one experiment they infected mice with a parasite that is known to induce those same effects—heightened anxiety and reduced activity of the BDNF gene in the brain. When they then introduced *Bifidobacterium longum*—another early colonizer of the gut after birth—into the mice, the parasite's effects disappeared. Somehow gut microbes seemed to be helping out the rodents' brain.

Gut bacteria are notoriously difficult to study, however. Not only are researchers mostly dependent on animal models, even creating the conditions needed to test those animals can be extremely tricky. Raising rodents free of microbes requires special facilities and equipment. In addition, labs can differ in the bacteria that inhabit their normal, or control, mice. These variations in difficult-to-track microscopic conditions can lead to seemingly conflicting results. The overall message, however, is that gastrointestinal microbes can change animals' emotional responses, although whether those results are positive or negative may depend on the environment both inside and surrounding the gut.

For example, Bienenstock, Foster, and their collaborators recently compared the behaviors of germ-free mice with normal mice. These germ-free mice were *less* anxious than the control rodents. They also saw brain changes to match those outcomes—namely, more expression of the gene encoding BDNF in the germ-free mice and fewer receptors for the neurotransmitters serotonin in the hippocampus and glutamate in the amygdala, a brain region that processes emotions. Serotonin is a key player in mood. Glutamate, like BDNF, is critical to learning and memory, suggesting that gut bacteria might have some effect on cognitive processes beyond mood. Yet when the researchers then tried to introduce microbes into adult germ-free mice, they observed no changes to behavior. This finding implies that the microbes exert their effects during a limited developmental time window. A second, similar study of theirs, using a different microbe, found altered expression of the genes relating to another important neurotransmitter, GABA, throughout the brain. The receptors for this chemical are a target for a class of drugs commonly used to treat anxiety, including Valium.

To get a more fine-grained view, the researchers dissected a mouse's myenteric plexus, a major component of the gut's nerve network. They inserted microelectrodes into individual neurons to record the cells' responses to various bacteria. These recordings revealed that some strains of *Bifidobacterium* and *Lactobacillus*, among the most prevalent bacterial species in the human gut, could block those neurons from producing impulses and lower the rodent's visible response to abdominal pain.

Bienenstock and his colleagues speculated that these neural changes might reach the brain by way of the vagus nerve. Indeed, severing this nerve in rodents abolished the microbes' effects. A second possible line of communication has also emerged in preliminary results presented at the Microbes for Health symposium in Paris last December: some strains of gut bacteria produce short-chain fatty acids that can increase the permeability of the blood-brain barrier. These molecules might alter which substances in the bloodstream can enter the brain.

As strong as the connection may seem in rodents, similar experiments in humans are lacking, leaving many open questions about what those intestinal interlopers might be doing in more complex organisms. "The findings are intriguing, but the details of what will generalize to humans requires detailed further study," Knight says. "We know that microbes influence gene expression in many tissues, so it would be a surprise if the brain were an exception." Emeran Mayer, a professor of neurogastroenterology at the David Geffen School of Medicine, U.C.L.A., is more hesitant. Researchers do not have the opportunity to raise babies in sterile environments, nor is our nervous system as simple as a rat's. "Given the robustness of the effects, one would expect that some of them also occur in humans, particularly in the early life periods," he says.

"But there is a major difference between the rodent and human brain–they do not have our extensive prefrontal cortex."

Probiotics for Your Brain

Evidence supporting a connection between gut ecology and the human brain is now trickling in. One example comes from infants–colicky babies have less diversity in their gut microbiota than is normal at that age and seem to be predisposed to stress later on. Other data are emerging from clinical trials of probiotic supplements–the microorganism-filled tablets and cultures, such as those added to yogurt, that are believed to aid digestion.

In 2011 French researchers published the results of a small clinical trial examining the antianxiety effects of probiotics. They had 66 patients take either a placebo or a probiotic formulation containing *Lactobacillus helveticus* and *B. longum*, two common inhabitants of guts, for a month. The participants were evaluated for anxiety and depression according to widely accepted checklists at the beginning and again at the end of the experiment. At the end of the month the group that took the probiotics showed the greatest decrease in signs of psychological distress as measured through the participants' self-reports.

Those findings are in line with what others have observed. In a paper currently in press, Mayer and his U.C.L.A. colleague Kirsten Tillisch worked with 45 healthy female volunteers to assess the effects of taking a probiotic formulation for a month. They divided the participants into three groups: 13 subjects were given a probiotic dairy product, another group received a milk-based, nonfermented dairy product, and the remaining women took nothing. When they scanned each woman's brain, they found that compared with the two control groups, the participants given probiotics had significantly less resting- state activity–the brain's firing patterns when thinking about nothing in particular–as well as a dampened response in their arousal networks, which includes the amygdala, in response to emotional faces. "We have several other studies either ongoing or in the planning phase all aimed at investigating if chronic probiotic intake or reduction of gut microbes by antibiotics can alter human brain structure and function," Mayer says.

Ultimately the concept of the gut-brain connection will very likely prove too simplistic. A fuller understanding of the effect of microorganisms on the psychological landscape will take into account chatter among other organs and systems in the body and their respective microbial communities. For example, acne has long been associated with anxiety and depression, and in 1930 dermatologists John Stokes and Donald Pillsbury put forward the "gut-brain-skin axis" hypothesis to explain the link. They proposed that emotional states might alter gut microbiota, which could increase the gut's permeability and lead to skin inflammation. They also advocated a probiotic remedy—a milk preparation containing *Lactobacillus acidophilus*, the common additive in dairy products. Bienenstock's group recently found evidence for this idea, showing that *Lactobacillus* soothes skin inflamed by stress and restores normal hair growth in mice.

We may yet discover that the microbes on our skin can communicate with those in our gut to influence our behavior. "It's not unreasonable to think that microbes elsewhere are involved," Bienenstock says. "Could we have some microbial ointment that improves health and well-being? The mind boggles at the possibilities."

About the Author

Moheb Costandi is a neurobiologist-turned-science-writer based in the UK. His blog, Neurophilosophy, is hosted by the Guardian *newspaper.*

You Know Those Parasites That Control Our Brains?

By Bradley van Paridon

If you believe the headlines, sixty percent of us may be infected with a parasite that changes behaviour. *Toxoplasma*, a natural parasite of cats, is said to cause rage, impulsiveness, and even mental illness. Most people only know *Toxoplasma* as the reason pregnant ladies aren't supposed to clean kitty litter. In recent times, though, this parasite has garnered quite a reputation as a mind-controlling zombie parasite. A reputation that may in fact be slightly exaggerated.

Rest assured the mind control phenomenon does exist in nature; I myself have been studying a different mind controlling parasite, *Dicrocoelium dendriticum*, over the course of my Ph.D. What most people don't realize though is that us scientists have little idea how exactly these parasites hijack their hosts. In most cases researchers must determine if the parasite is in fact willfully controlling the host by assessing the evolutionary value of the trait.

The most common instances of manipulation occur when a parasite must be eaten by the next host in the life cycle. In the case of the organism I study this involves making the leap from an ant into a grazing mammal. Because deer don't tend to search out and eat ants the parasite hijacks an ant and forces it to climb and cling to plants; which grazing mammals do eat. There they wait until something comes along and gobbles them up along with the plant they are on. Even more spectacular is the fact the parasite turns the behaviour on and off. When temperatures rise and the clinging ants are in danger of overheating the parasite relinquishes control but as soon as the temperature cools they come straight back, sometimes to the exact flower they left.

It seems like a no brainer that the parasite must be controlling the ants but a careful examination of the behaviour in question needs to be undertaken in lieu of finding the chemical or mechanical means it may be using. First the parasite must have a reason to manipulate the host. In the above example this would be the need to move from an ant into a grazer. Next, any behaviour being changed by a parasite should act to achieve the desired outcome and only occur in infected individuals. Again looking at the *Dicrocoelium* example we can see that the clinging behaviour shown only by infected ants will in fact increase their exposure to grazing mammals. The story of *Toxoplasma*'s alleged behaviour manipulation doesn't quite meet these criteria.

The story begins with the unique relationship between *Toxoplasma* and cats. *Toxoplasma* infects not just cats but everything from lizards to humans and they all become infected in one of three ways: 1) coming into contact with the parasite offspring in cat feces 2) eating infected meat or 3) from one's mother while in the womb. Due to a quirk of biology, though, it is only within cats that *Toxoplasma* completes sexual reproduction. This is why cats are the only ones to shed *Toxoplasma* in their poop and why pregnant ladies shouldn't go near said poop. It has long been theorized that *Toxoplasma* should prefer being in cats due to the benefits of sexual reproduction. Sex mixes the gene pool, which benefits a population by creating novel gene combinations that drive evolution. This in theory is the reason *Toxoplasma* would manipulate a host to enter cats. Many believed they confirmed this theory when infected rodents started to display some odd behaviours. Since then a slew of studies have claimed that *Toxoplasma* influences behaviour, including studies famously investigating humans. It wasn't until a lab from Australia started digging through these studies that anyone questioned the claims.

The original work on rodents stated infected hosts showed reduced movement and anxiety plus a remarkable attraction to the smell of cat urine. This definitely seems like something the parasite might induce to increase the chances it gets eaten. Upon closer inspection, however, the criteria necessary to conclude *Toxoplasma* has evolved the trait of manipulation are not fully met. Many studies report either no effects on behaviour or changes to behaviours that have no bearing on the chances of being eaten by a cat. Behaviours like social interactions or dominance. This casts doubt onto the idea that *Toxoplasma* evolved the adaptive trait of mind control. Rather it looks like some rodents with parasites sometimes do weird things. Plus there is another species of parasite, *Eimeria veriformis*, that also causes an attraction to cat urine in mice, but this parasite dies if eaten by a cat offering no advantage to manipulation.

What then of the presumed benefit of cat hosts? Is it really enough that selection would favour the mind control trait? Again, upon closer inspection maybe not. The genetic profile of *Toxoplasma* populations globally appears to be a predominantly asexual one. There is little genetic mixing and only three main lineages dominate in Europe and North America. Meaning the parasite seems to be doing fine without having sex in cats and is being transmitted via the food chain or from mother to offspring. *Toxoplasma* certainly hasn't had a problem invading many environments including those with a distinct lack of cats. Beluga whales in the arctic are infected and now pose a health risk to Inuit people who eat them. And foxes too on cat free islands off the coast of Norway now carry *Toxoplasma*.

Finally we must now question the bold claims that *Toxoplasma* causes aberrant behaviours in humans. In the largest study to date looking for the top reported behaviour changes in humans, things like impulsiveness, anxiety, depression, and mental illness, no correlation between infection and behaviour was found.

The ability of parasites to manipulate hosts is one of the most fascinating areas of biological research. As the *Toxoplasma* story illustrates, though, it is very easy to attribute a potential quirk in behaviour to a highly specialized parasite gaining control over its host. Not all hope is lost, though, for *Toxoplasma*'s master manipulator reputation. New research into the potential mechanisms used to influence behaviour may discover the smoking gun that definitively implicates *Toxoplasma*. Although this research isn't yet producing headlines about zombie parasites, this is exactly the research the field needs. And it may ultimately yield the best headlines of all. "Key to mind control found" or "Zombie gene discovered by parasite researchers." Now that should move some magazines.

About the Author

Bradley van Paridon is a Ph.D. student studying parasitology at the University of Lethbridge and a member of the NSERC CREATE Host Parasite Interactions Group.

Section 4: Monsters in Nature

Blood Ties: Vampire Bats Build Trust to Become Food-Sharing Pals

By Jason G. Goldman

For vampire bats, the mark of true friendship is breaking bread–er, blood–together. These animals require their liquid meals to survive, and they require them often. If one misses a feeding just three nights in a row, it could starve to death. So the creatures have developed a friendly way to cope: sometimes well-fed bats regurgitate blood directly into the mouths of hungry companions. That blood may not be enough for a full meal, but it lets the recipient live and hunt another day. Now new research has tapped into the secrets of how vampire bats form these intimate bonds.

Plenty of animal parents regurgitate food for their offspring, but this kind of food sharing between unrelated adults is nearly unheard of in the animal kingdom, says Ohio State University behavioral ecologist Gerald G. Carter. Biologists have long wondered how such relationships form in the first place and how vampire bats maintain them, especially because the animals involved are not kin. Some unrelated bats have been seen traveling together for more than a decade.

"You could be investing time and energy helping a partner, but if they don't cooperate with you, you could be worse off than if you never engaged at all," Carter explains. "If you're in that situation, what's the best strategy for mitigating risk?" He is lead author on a new study of these bats' cooperation, published Thursday in *Current Biology*.

About two decades ago, researchers put forth a hypothesis of animal social behavior called the "raising the stakes" model. It proposes that one individual begins by making small, low-cost investments in the relationship. If they are reciprocated, the animal gradually escalates to larger, higher-risk investments. If the relationship does not go well, it tries somebody new. "I think that's a really intuitive idea for how individuals would form relationships, but it hasn't really been tested properly," Carter says.

To assess this hypothesis, Carter and his team trapped about 30 wild vampire bats from two different, unrelated colonies in Panama and then introduced pairs of unfamiliar bats to each other in the lab. Some of the animals quickly began grooming the stranger they were partnered with–just a little bit. In some pairs, grooming eventually gave way to food sharing. The latter was relatively rare, and it was always preceded by grooming, a much lower-cost investment. The amount of grooming rose sharply in the days just before the first instance of food sharing, and then it plateaued afterward. The researchers say these observations provide the first empirical support for the raising the stakes hypothesis.

"[This] study makes the point that reciprocity is not some cold calculation of tit for tat but ultimately rests on trust that is built up over time," says Emory University primatologist Frans de Waal, who was not involved in the new paper. "It is part of an emotional, close relationship, as is also speculated for the primates. Grooming among primates may do the same as in the bats: prepare relationships for occasions when mutual assistance is truly needed." Carter agrees, noting that even after the bats were returned to the wild, many maintained the relationships they initially formed in captivity.

Carter suggests that this kind of study might help biologists better understand human relationships as well. "The quality and quantity of the social bonds you have with others is really important for your health, for your reproduction, for your survival," he says. "But nobody really understands how you get relationships: How much is luck? How much is personality? This is the next frontier, I think."

About the Author

Jason G. Goldman is a science journalist based in Los Angeles. He has written about animal behavior, wildlife biology, conservation, and ecology for Scientific

American, Los Angeles *magazine, the* Washington Post, *the* Guardian, *the BBC,* Conservation *magazine, and elsewhere. He contributes to* Scientific American's *"60-Second Science" podcast and is co-editor of* Science Blogging: The Essential Guide *(Yale University Press). He enjoys sharing his wildlife knowledge on television and on the radio, and often speaks to the public about wildlife and science communication.*

Pharaohs Got Yummy Mummy Meals

By Cynthia Graber

Ancient Egyptian mummies were carefully embalmed and entombed with golden jewelry, furniture, and clothing. And to make sure they did not go hungry on their travels, they were also buried with mummified *meat.* King Tut was accompanied by 48 wooden cases that held a variety of cattle and poultry joints prepared for dinner.

Archaeologists have known about this penchant for after-death munchies, but they didn't understand how the meat was treated. So researchers in Egypt and in the U.K. examined samples from both the Cairo and the British Museums.

They extracted balm from meat samples and their wrappers. The meat included beef ribs and a calf some 2,000 years old. The wrapping contained fats that did not touch the calf, suggesting a balm applied only to the wrap. The rib dinner showed evidence of beeswax and a luxury item called Pistacia resin. The study was published in the *Proceedings of the National Academy of Sciences.* [Katherine A. Clark, Salima Ikram, and Richard P. Evershed, Organic chemistry of balms used in the preparation of pharaonic meat mummies.]

The scientists say their findings show that ancient Egyptians paid as much exquisite attention to embalming and preserving meat as they did to humans and pet animals. Because one should always pack a meal for a long journey.

Your Average, Everyday Zombie

By Christie Wilcox

"The purpose of man's life...is to become an abject zombie who serves a purpose he does not know, for reasons he is not to question."
–Ayn Rand

Of all the cryptic, creepy, and cruel creatures that emerge each Halloween, few captivate our imaginations like the living dead. Sure, they look dreadful, smell bad, and have the conversational skills of a well-adjusted slug, but despite their bad manners and constant lust for our brains, zombies have clawed their way into our hearts. It just wouldn't be Halloween without them.

Like any good monster, the legend of the zombie is based in truth. According to Voodoo traditions, powerful spiritual men called Bokors have the power to kill a man and then raise him from the dead, turning him into a *zombi*, a mindless slave to the Bokor who created him. As outsiders began to look into the myths, they discovered that these sinister sorcerers use a chemical cocktail, including the deadly poison tetrodotoxin, to mimic the physiological signs of death. This zombi juice doesn't just slow the victim's heart rate–the toxic mix has lasting effects on the human brain including memory loss and delirium, making them ideal slaves. Once the target is declared dead and buried, the Bokor can dig up the grave and claim his zombi.

While Bokors have been tinkering with brain chemistry to make the perfect zombie for hundreds of years, there are others that have been perfecting the art of zombification for much longer. Parasites are the Victor Frankensteins of the natural world. These mini-neuroscientists turn other creatures into mindless slaves, serving only to further the master's selfish goals. They do that voodoo better than we do, and they have for eons.

In all of the cases I'm about to present, once the host is infected, they are the living dead. They have no hope of recovery, no chance for redemption. They will perform their acts as needed by their parasitic Bokor, and only once their bodies have served their function will the zombie be released into the sweet arms of eternity.

The Zombie, It Stings

While they might lack the lust for brains, parasitic wasps are the masters of neurological zombification. The emerald cockroach wasp, for example, turns its cockroach host into an ill-fated nanny. With carefully placed stings that inject a venom cocktail into the roach's brain, the wasp puts the roach into a zombie-like state where it happily follows its attacker to a dark chamber underground. The wasp then lays her eggs in the complacent roach and seals it in its tomb. Soon enough, the eggs hatch, eat, pupate, and emerge while the cockroach sits and waits for its body to be consumed.

But perhaps it is the parasitic wasp *Cotesia glomerata* that most deserves the title of master. Females lay their eggs in unsuspecting caterpillars. When the larvae hatch, they literally eat their host from the inside out. But even more incredible is the caterpillar's reaction to such usury: the hapless host transforms into an undead bodyguard, protecting the young wasps even after they have gorged themselves on the caterpillar's internal organs. The mostly-eaten victim will even spin a silk web over the pupated wasps that just feasted on its flesh, a final act of devotion to its Bokors, before it dies. What chemical spell the larvae cast on their host to instill such loyalty remains a mystery.

Fly Me to the Grave

They might look like fruit flies, but Phorid flies are more than just a harmless pest–at least to the ants that serve as host for the fly's larvae. Phorid flies are the ideal Hollywood zombie parasite, complete with a hunger for neurological tissue. Gruesome as they might be, you gotta give the flies points for style.

First, the momma fly injects her eggs into the body cavity of the ant host. Once they hatch, the larvae make their way to the ant's head, where they feed on hemolymph (ant blood), muscle, and nervous tissue (aka brraaaaaiiiiiinnnnssss). The larval flies will spend weeks inside the head of their host, controlling its behavior while snacking on its brains until they have completely emptied the ant's head. The ant, meanwhile, wanders around in a zombie-like state. When the young fly decides it is ready to pupate, it releases an enzyme that decapitates the ant by dissolving the membrane that attaches its head to its body. The larva pupates in the ant's disembodied head for about two more weeks, then emerges as a full-grown adult, ready to mate and find its own zombie host.

Other flies turn wasps into murderous zombie queens. *Xenos vesparum* larvae wait patiently until a wasp lands close by. When it senses its victim, the larva leaps onto the wasp and burrows through its exoskeleton into its abdomen, and begins feasting on the wasp's blood. As it grows, the larva starts to mess with the wasp's mind. The normally social wasp withdraws from its colony, and starts to act recklessly. Then, in early summer, the infected wasp just leaves its colony behind, and as if under some spell, travels to a meeting place. Soon, other parasitized wasps arrive, and the parasites begin to mate. The male flies emerge from the wasps and seek out the females that remain in their zombie hosts, granting the men access to the only part needed for reproduction.

The wasps that were lucky enough to be infected by male flies die. Those infected with females, though, are still under the control of their parasites. They begin to act like wasp queens, gathering food and gaining weight. They then travel to sites where queens gather in the fall, and spend the winter in the lap of luxury among other wasp royalty. When the seasons change and the wasps emerge, the zombie queens go back to their colonies, carrying their deadly load of fly larvae. Everywhere they travel, larvae are left behind, waiting for the next unsuspecting wasp to land.

Rosemary's Baby Barnacle

Most parasites are really, really small. But not all zombifying parasites are itsy-bitsy. Take, for example, the Rhizocephalans–the parasitic barnacles.

Yes, I did just say parasitic *barnacle*, although they don't look much like barnacles as adults. The adult parasites look like a sac where a female crab would have eggs. It's classified as a barnacle, however, due to its larval forms, specifically the cypris larvae, which neatly place it in the class Cirripedia.

The barnacle's strategy is simple: find a crab. Stop her from shedding so she can't get rid of you. Tap into her nervous and circulatory systems and get comfortable. Grow. Sterilize her, so nothing competes for your living space. As you get too big to fit inside, pretend to be an egg sac. Have her bathe you in water, take gentle care of you, and feed you nutrients because she thinks she's pregnant. She'll even help you spread your larvae like they're her own eggs by fanning them into the water.

However, there is an obvious problem. Not every crab is female, and thus predisposed to tending its eggs. So what does the parasite do when it accidentally infects a male crab instead? Well, it's simple, really. It makes it act like a woman.

By altering hormones in the male crab's neurophysiology, it causes the male crab to act like a female one. Its abdomen flattens and widens, and it starts taking on the behavioral traits of a pregnant female. The male goes through the same process of nurturing and caring for its wee little parasite babies that the female would. The big boy will continue to love, adore, and feed its little parasitic baby until he dies, just like a girl crab would.

Swimming with the Fishes

Spinochordodes tellinii, also known as a hairworm, are free-living aquatic organisms as adults, who, as nematodes, eek out an existence in the mud. Their young, though, thrive on the flesh of crickets.

Problem is, crickets don't always hang around wet places, and if the nematode were to leave its host when it's somewhere high and dry, it would die. What better way to ensure that it ends up where it wants to be than to drive the unwitting cricket host to suicide by drowning?

How exactly the worm controls the cricket's brain is unknown, but theories suggest that the parasite has developed a way to mimic natural chemical signals in the bug's brain. Analysis of the compounds of infested brains reveals heightened levels of neurotransmitters and chemicals responsible for movement and orientation, particularly with relation to gravity. These proteins are similar to the ones produced by the insect, but are not naturally occurring, suggesting that the parasite is able to produce and excrete its own chemical signals to screw with the cricket's mind. The end result of which, much to the parasite's joy, is that the cricket seeks out water and hops right in. More often than not, the act is fatal—crickets are terrible swimmers, and most who leap into the cool depths drown. This assisted suicide gives the parasite the chance to break free and wiggle its way easily down to the mud, where it continues its life cycle.

More Than a Fluke

Trematodes, or flukes, are known for their complex life cycles that involve multiple hosts. Often, switching from host to host is facilitated by predatory interactions. *Dicroelium dentriticum*, a trematode that lives in the livers of sheep, is no exception. The trouble is, its intermediate host is an ant, and sheep aren't generally known for their hunger for ants. So how does a parasitic fluke get from an ant to a sheep?

Well, actually, it starts with a snail. The snail accidentally eats the fluke's eggs while going along its merry snail way, and the parasite hatches and develops in the snail's gonads. Eventually, the fluke is excreted in the snail's slime, which is conveniently eaten by an ant. This is where things get weird. Once infected, the ant continues about its business as normal–for the most part. By day the ant acts like an ant. But as the sun goes down, the parasite takes over. Every night, the zombie ant will leave its colony behind and search for a blade of grass. When it finds one, it climbs to the top, bites down, and waits until sunrise. Night after night, the ant will dutifully wait atop its blade until it gets accidentally eaten by a grazing sheep, thus completing its enslaver's life cycle.

Who Said Zombies Aren't Fungis?

Even microscopic fungi get in on the zombifying trend. The fungus *Ophiocordyceps unilateralis* is yet another zombifying parasite targeting ants (they really get the short end of the zombie stick). It's all well and good to target ants, but a bit of a dilemma for the fungus arose from its choice of host: the fungus needs the perfect combination of light, humidity, and temperature to survive, and those conditions don't exist on the ground. Ants generally live on the ground, and thus shouldn't be good housing for *Ophiocordyceps*. Not to worry, though–the fungus has engineered a mind-altering solution.

Ants infected with *Ophiocordyceps unilateralis* find themselves compelled to amble far from their homes, climb trees or sprouts, and end up on the bottom side of a leaf where they clamp down their jaws and wait while the fungus eats them from the inside out. What's incredible is the precision with which these zombied ants choose their final resting place: they all choose to die on the vein on the bottom of a north-facing leaf approximately 25 cm above the ground in an area with 94 to 95 percent humidity and between 20 and 30 degrees Celsius–perfect conditions for the fungus to grow. After a few weeks, spores fall from the now fully eaten corpse to infect other ants and continue the fungus' life cycle.

About the Author

Christie Wilcox is a postdoctoral researcher in cellular and molecular biology at the University of Hawaii, where she studies venom. She is also a science blogger and communicator.

Zombie Creatures: What Happens When Animals Are Possessed by a Parasitic Puppet Master?

By Katherine Harmon

A spider, seemingly possessed, spins an uncharacteristic web—just before wasp larvae nesting on its abdomen suck the last nourishing juices from the spider's dying body and make a cocoon in the weird web.

A worm gets into the brain of a shy, shade-loving snail, compelling it to crawl out of its safe home and into the open where it gets attacked by a bird—which is destined to be the parasite's next host.

Creepy tales like these are happening all over the animal kingdom, and not just on Halloween or under a full moon. Some organisms have taken evolutionary advantage to a whole new level, achieving success by insidiously—and still quite mysteriously—changing the behavior of another animal against its will.

Although not undead in the strictest sci-fi definition of "zombie," these captive creatures nonetheless behave as if possessed by a force from beyond. That force, however, is often controlling them from the inside, making the unfortunate hosts do deadly things.

In the case of the spooked spider (*Plesiometa argyra*), a parasitic wasp (*Hymenoepimecis argyraphaga*) lays her eggs on the spider's abdomen. Just before the larva emerges, the host spins a strange, new type of web—one that looks nothing like its usual wide nets. This silk platform, however, is perfectly suited to supporting a cocoon for the vulnerable young wasp larvae, which have been feasting on the spider's innards as they grow.

The snail-manipulating flatworm (*Leucochloridium paradoxum*) grows and multiplies inside the snail. Once ready to move on to its next host, the worms push up into the snail's tentacles, making them swell and squirm, mimicking the action of bugs that birds like to eat. As the snail crawls, blindly, into the sunlight, a passing bird is likely to swoop down to snatch a tasty tentacle or two. The worm-infested meal will then infect the bird, which passes it onto other snails via dubious droppings.

The mechanisms by which these parasites are commanding their hosts remain, by in large, unsolved mysteries.

"We don't know how it works, but it's obviously some type of chemical," says David Hughes, a researcher at Harvard University. "It's co-opting a preexisting behavior." As part of their normal routine, snails climb stalks and spiders spin webs, but the parasites have managed to take these particular behaviors and mold them to their own advantage—often resulting in their hosts' demise.

"Typically you have behavior that a host would do at some point in its life," adds Edward Levri, an associate professor of biology at the Pennsylvania State University in Altoona. "It's just happening at an odd, nonadvantageous time for the host, to the benefit of the parasite."

Creepy Control

So many very different—and very bizarre—examples of parasite-controlled behavior modification have been observed that researchers have a wealth of instances to study. But it is no longer enough to document these parasites. "We have to go beyond describing behavior," Hughes says. "Now people are trying to look at *how* parasites are changing behavior."

Figuring this puzzle out, however, has proved to be quite difficult. "Modified organisms are more complex than we had previously believed," says Frederic Thomas, a scientist at the Genetics and Evolution of Infectious Diseases research group in Montpellier, France, and the department of biology at the University of Montreal.

With improved technology, researchers in this freaky field have been able to start sequencing the genomes and parsing proteins of some of these parasites and hosts to unravel where behavioral changes happen. "In at least some cases, some of these parasites produce neurotransmitters or hormones that mimic host hormones," Levri says.

Not all of the parasites, however, are traditional body snatchers.

"You can easily understand that a parasite can control the behavior when it is inside," Thomas says. But how do some manage to dictate a host's behavior when they're not, technically, hosting a parasite? "To me, it's like magic," he adds.

The aberrant web-spinning *P. argyra* demonstrates this to some extent, the parasitic wasp eggs having been laid on the outside of the spider's body. In another bizarre example of external control, a different species of wasp (*Ampulex compressa*) is able to control a cockroach–via an injection into its brain–and force it to enter its nest to become food and shelter for the wasp's larvae.

Are Humans Next?

Even people may not be fully immune to such manipulation. Much of our modern-day behavior seems to suit the interests of other species, such as hitchhiking invasive species and airline-riding viruses that hop continents in a matter of hours. But can we also be manipulated from within?

To a certain degree, yes. Perhaps the most familiar example is rabies, which can cause human hosts–like other mammals–to salivate excessively, thereby spreading the deadly virus. Researchers have even shown that malaria-infected people are more attractive to mosquitoes, which spread the infected blood to another host, according to a 2005 *PLoS ONE* paper.

Such pernicious parasitism is indeed widespread throughout various kingdoms. "We know it's evolved a few times," Exeter's Hughes says. So, he wonders: "Has it been different solutions to the same problem?"

In the quest to understand both how these uncanny behaviors work and how they emerged, researchers are also enlisting the help of evolutionary ecology. They are examining these behaviors on a smaller scale. For example if two larvae are growing on a controlled host, like the *P. argyra* orb-web spider, what happens to the spider's behavior when one is mature and the other isn't yet ready to emerge?

Some hosts have evolved to cope with frequent parasitism. For example, one beetle that is frequently killed off early by a parasite has adapted by increasing its sexual activity and producing more offspring, Thomas notes.

But the chilling question remains: How can bugs control other bugs? And in some of the more extreme examples, Hughes ponders: "How can a member of one kingdom modify the behavior of another kingdom?" Until scientists find that answer, it's all eerie action, for sure.

How This Zombie Fungus Turns Cicadas into Horror-Movie Sex Bots

By Rachel Nuwer

Matt Kasson, a forest pathologist and mycologist at West Virginia University, has spent the past week chasing cicadas across northern Virginia. Each night he has watched pale nymphs emerge from the earth like ghostly apparitions and then make their way into trees, where they will soon molt to become winged adults.

Both the cicadas and Kasson have been waiting for this moment–but not for the same reason. After 17 years underground, billions of Brood X periodical cicadas, as the insects are known, are emerging into the light across the eastern U.S. this year to find mates and launch the next generation. Kasson, on the other hand, has come for an equally awe-inspiring yet very different facet of one of nature's most epic life cycles: "the big fungal show," as he puts it. It is one wild performance in which a parasitic fungus turns some of the insects into singled-minded sex machines–after causing their genitals to fall off. The phenomenon is well documented, but scientists such as Kasson are working to figure out *how* the freaky fungus hijacks its host.

An estimated 3,000 species of cicadas live around the world, and a diversity of parasitic fungi have evolved alongside them. Kasson studies one exceptionally peculiar species called *Massospora cicadina*. It only infects so-called periodical cicadas such as Brood X–those that emerge every 13 or 17 years.

M. cicadina's spores have also patiently spent the past 17 years in the soil, awaiting the Brood X nymphs. The immature insects become infected when they come into contact with the spores on their way to the surface, and the fungus grows out of sight for the first seven to 10 days as its host molts into an adult.

After that deceptive period of quiet, however, the infection begins to manifest–with horrifying results. Males' abdominal plates begin to slough off, revealing a chalky white plug made of fungal spores. The spores can come off when an insect walks or flies. But mostly, they spread through sex attempts.

Healthy male cicadas sing to attract females, which indicate their receptiveness to mating by flicking their wings. A female unfortunate enough to fall for an infected male's siren song will not only fail to get her eggs fertilized (the male's genitals have long since fallen off) but will also become infected herself, essentially making *M. cicadina* a sexually transmitted disease.

Infected females' abdomen tends to remain more or less intact because they have stronger muscular tissue in place for laying eggs. But that does not mean females have it easy. If a male mates with an infected female, her fungus-ridden genitalia usually break off—and get carried away by the male. "Basically, the male has this permanent ornament attached to him with a legacy of deeds past done," Kasson says. Some infected males also flick their wings like a female, attracting other hapless males that become infected when they attempt to mate.

Much of Kasson's research entails figuring out how in the world the fungus compels cicadas to become sexual zombies for spreading its spores. In 2019 he and his colleagues reported in *Fungal Ecology* that one compound in particular, cathinone, seems to be key for turning *M. cicadina*–infected hosts into sexual automatons. Now, in Virginia, he is screening cicadas for fungal infections, looking for sample insects to study in the lab. "Also," Kasson adds, "I have to admit I wasn't going to miss the opportunity to just spend time with Brood X."

Cathinone is a well-known, naturally occurring stimulant in the amphetamine family. Scientists had previously pinpointed it as an active ingredient in khat, a plant native to the Horn of Africa and the Arabian Peninsula, where people sometimes chew it for a buzz. Synthetic cathinone is also a key component in pharmaceuticals prescribed for attention deficit hyperactivity disorder and in illegal drugs called "bath salts." "We aren't seeing face-eating cicadas," Kasson says, referring to a notorious 2012 Florida incident that media reports blamed on bath salts. "But we can learn something about how the fungus might be working from what these medicines are used for."

Medications that contain synthetic cathinone, for example, can suppress appetite and increase the ability to focus. So it is possible the fungus alters host behavior to its advantage by making cicadas single-mindedly pursue mating rather than feeding or resting—thus spreading the spores to more mates.

Interestingly, Kasson and other researchers have also found evidence of psilocybin—the psychedelic ingredient in magic mushrooms—in another *Massospora* species that only infects annual cicadas in the western U.S. "Psilocybin and amphetamines are obviously two very different types of drugs, but we think these alkaloids could be having a bit of redundancy in the ability to suppress appetite, increase stamina, and prolong wakefulness," Kasson says.

He suspects that the presence of these compounds in *Massospora* species represents an example of convergent evolution, in which a feature independently evolves in different species to perform a similar function. Cathinone's occurrence in khat plants, however, does raise one intriguing question: Could these plants contain hidden fungal partners that are actually the engineers behind the compounds? As Kasson points out, this would not be the first time that credit for a plant's apparent psychoactive properties turned out to belong to a fungus: in 2004 scientists discovered that an LSD-like compound found in morning glory was not produced by the plant itself but by a fungus that lives inside it.

Kasson hopes to further investigate this and other questions in future studies. In particular, he would like to dose healthy cicadas directly with cathinone to see how it alters their behavior. He is also interested in looking at the dozen or so other *Massospora* species out there to see what interesting compounds they may hold—something that could even be useful for pharmaceutical drug discovery.

Speaking of drugs, however, Kasson emphasizes that people looking to get high should not turn to infected cicadas—something that he has been concerned to see discussed in online forums. It would take hundreds or even thousands of cicadas to produce a dose high enough to have an effect on humans, he says. And cicadas also contain more than 1,000 other compounds, some of them known toxins. "You'd have to eat an awful lot of cicadas to have some effect from the amphetamine that's in there," agrees Chris Simon, a phylogeneticist at the University of Connecticut. "You'd be sick long before you ate enough."

That said, both Simon and Kasson say people should not worry much about pets or kids coming into contact with infected cicadas. For starters, it may be difficult to find them. Only about 5 percent of cicadas tend to be infected in the first place. And although Brood X consists of billions of insects, they are dispersed over a large geographical area. "I wouldn't lick one myself," Kasson says. "But if your animal eats one or two infected cicadas, that's not going to be a problem."

About the Author

Rachel Nuwer is a freelance journalist and author of Poached: Inside the Dark World of Wildlife Trafficking *(Da Capo Press, 2018). She lives in Brooklyn, N.Y.*

Zombie Cicadas' Bodies Are Literally Falling Apart

By Jennifer Frazer

Author's note: This blog post is rated not safe for lunch. Actually, it's rated not safe for breakfast, lunch, dinner, or teatime. I debated whether I should even write it it's so revolting but a friend who reports for KUNC convinced me I should. So...blame public radio.

The opening line of a new paper in *Scientific Reports* reads, "Parasites and their hosts cohabit the same body, but they have strongly divergent interests in how to make use of it,"–to which I instantly thought, "like any married couple in a car."

Only in this case, one spouse is actively trying to kill the other.

Such is the case for the fungus *Massospora cicadina* and its hapless victim, the periodical cicada (*Magicicada* sp.). North Americans have a love-hate (some would say hate-hate) relationship with this plump insect, which has a bizarre habit of emerging en masse every 13 or 17 years to eat, mate, and drive area humans to distraction with their shrill, 100-decibel screeching. What can you do? If life gives you cicadas, make cicada ice cream.

When I was about seven or eight a brood emerged around us in northern Kentucky. I had endless fun plucking the adults off their perches by pinching their wings–they were docile like cows, so you could walk right up to them–and studying the fat, red-eyed insects. I do not recall seeing any that were horrifically maimed. But as it turns out, there is one parasite that has adapted to the periodical cicada life cycle, waiting patiently in the soil for 13 or 17 years for their victims to emerge. This is *Massospora cicadina*, and it makes its own version of cicada ice cream.

Cicada nymphs live underground for those 13 or 17 years, sucking the juices from plant roots. When the magic moment comes and they burrow to the surface, some of them come into contact with spores of the fungus. About two to five percent of them end up infected.

After finding its way inside its shiny new cicada, the fungus makes itself right at home by multiplying mercilessly into thousands of white, powdery spores. These spores are conidia, asexually-produced reproductive cells, and are termed a Stage I infection. These spores are infectious to other adult cicadas.

Cicadas infected by conidia experience a similar infection, termed Stage II, that results in sexually-produced spores. These spores are meant to find their way to the soil, where they can withstand more than a dozen years of environmental abuse as they await their next meal.

Cicadas infected by either kind of spore acquire an abdomen swollen with chalky white spores, ultimately causing both their reproductive equipment and several terminal segments of their body to fall off, leaving a gruesome open wound.

Of course, being cicadas, not only do they not grasp the horror of their situation, they have no idea they are infected or that they can infect other cicadas. So they also go on doing all the normal things cicadas do during their month topside. All the things.

Which produced this horrifying sentence, brought to you verbatim from the esteemed pages of Nature's own *Scientific Reports*, "...[T]hus, it is relatively common to find a healthy cicada with its genitalia plunged into the abdominal spore mass of an infected partner or to see healthy cicadas attached to fragments of abdomen or terminalia that have torn free from infected partners during attempted copulation."

Oh god.

Mating isn't the only thing infected cicadas do, of course. Cicadas infected by Stage I spores tend to drag their gaping abdomens behind them, leaving a trail of spores, not unlike (and I'm just not going to hold back today) a dog dealing with infected anal sacs. Cicadas infected with Stage II spores also do this, but "spend relatively more time than Stage I cicadas flying and visibly spewing spores from their damaged abdomens." Remember, the goal of Stage II spores is not to find another host, but to end up in soil likely to be home to baby cicadas.

But it gets worse. Because *Massospora* decided that all this just wasn't quite evil enough. It really needed to up the ante. So, as the scientists reveal in their graphic new paper, males who are infected with Stage I spores will respond to the mating calls of other males by flicking their wings–something only healthy, receptive females usually do. And, cicadas being cicadas, you can guess the result.

Thus, males are more likely to become infected than females because they will mate with infected females but also with infected males. But what if this was just a side effect of infection? What if something about having your entire abdomen filled with evil fungal spawn had some sort of generic feminizing effect?

The scientists thought about this possibility. But only males infected with Stage I spores flick their wings in response to male calls. Stage II infected males do not. If male wing-flicking was simply a side effect of being infected by *Massospora*, we would expect both types of infected males to behave this way. So it seems likely the behavior is an active fungal stratagem to improve its reproductive potential. There may be two organisms living in the cicada's body, but only one of them has their hands on the wheel, and it's not the cicada.

Massosspora has also been shown to manipulate the sexual behavior of at least one other non-periodical cicada, and more examples in other species are suspected. So, the authors conclude, to the general phenomenon of zombie insects whose behavior is manipulated by parasitic fungi (a large category mycologists refer to as entomophthoralean fungi), we may now add fungi that mess with insect bedroom behavior. As they say, all is fair in love and war. This is both.

Reference

John R. Cooley, David C. Marshall, Kathy B. R. Hill. A specialized fungal parasite (*Massospora cicadina*) hijacks the sexual signals of periodical cicadas (Hemiptera: Cicadidae: Magicicada). *Scientific Reports*, 2018; 8 (1) DOI: 10.1038/s41598-018-19813-0

About the Author

Jennifer Frazer, an AAAS Science Journalism Award–winning science writer, authored The Artful Amoeba blog for Scientific American. *She has degrees in biology, plant pathology, and science writing.*

Undead-End: Fungus That Controls Zombie-Ants Has Own Fungal Stalker

By Katherine Harmon

An unsuspecting worker ant in Brazil's rainforest leaves its nest one morning. But instead of following the well-worn treetop paths of its nest mates, this ant stumbles along clumsily, walking in aimless circles, convulsing from time to time.

At high noon, as if programmed, the ant plunges its mandibles into the juicy main vein of a leaf and soon dies. Within days the stem of a fungus sprouts from the dead ant's head. After growing a stalk, the fungus casts spores to the ground below, where they can be picked up by other passing ants.

This strange cycle of undead life and death has been well documented and has earned the culprit the moniker: "zombie-ant" fungus–even in the scientific literature. But scientists are just learning the intricacies of this interplay between the *Ophiocordyceps* parasitic fungus and the Camponotini carpenter ants that it infects. Fossil evidence implies that this zombifying infection might have been happening for at least 48 million years. Recent research also suggests that different species of the fungus might specialize to infect different groups of ants across the globe. And close examination of the infected ant corpses has revealed an even newer level of spooky savagery–other fungi often parasitize the zombie-ant fungus parasite itself.

"We have advanced a great deal in understanding how the fungus controls ant behavior," David Hughes, an assistant professor of entomology and biology at the Pennsylvania State University, says. Every few months scientists are discovering yet another peculiar trait that, added together, make this parasite one of the most insidious infections–or perhaps that honor goes to the parasite that ultimately kills the killer parasite.

Deadly Infection

This clever *Ophiocordyceps* fungus depends on ants to reproduce and spread, but it has found an abundant host animal. As Hughes notes, ants have been incredibly successful, currently comprising an estimated half of all insect biomass worldwide.

One of the first clues that a tropical carpenter ant has become infected with *Ophiocordyceps* is that it will leave the dry tree canopy and descend to the humid forest floor, staggering over debris and plants. "Infected ants behave as zombies," Hughes and his colleagues wrote in a 2011 *BMC Ecology* paper describing some of the latest findings. The ant will walk randomly, displaying "convulsions that make them fall down and thus preclude them from returning to the canopy," they noted, comparing the stumbling gait with a "drunkard's walk."

The clumsiness cannot, however, be blamed on the ant. "While the manipulated individual may look like an ant, it represents a fungal genome expressing fungal behavior through the body of an ant," the researchers noted in the paper. Hence the zombie designation.

Evans suggests that a nerve toxin spurred on by the fungus is at least partly to blame, "judging from the uncoordinated movements and hyperactivity of the ants infected," he says. Ants that have been dissected at this stage of infection reveal heads already full of fungal cells.

Eventually, an affected ant will stop on the underside of one leaf, roughly 25 centimeters from the forest floor, and clamp down on the leaf's main vein. (This position appears to be optimal for the fungus's later stage in which it ejects spores onto the soil directly below.) Biting leaves is not normal ant behavior. The zombies' bites are synchronized near noon (possibly cued by clock genes in the fungus) and usually occur in a north-northwestern orientation.

Scientists have found that the fungus also triggers atrophy in its victim's muscles–specifically those around its mandibles. This atrophy is prompted by metabolites that purge the muscle cells of mitochondria and sarcoplasmic reticulum (which provide energy and signals), according to the *BMC Ecology* research. Perhaps counterintuitively, when the infected ant bites onto the leaf vein in its so-called "death grip," this atrophy causes it to have lockjaw, leaving it there to die. This seemingly small detail is crucial to the fungus's success. "Without the death grip," Hughes explains, "the ant would fall to the ground," destroying the launching point for the fungus's spores.

By that stage, cells from the fungus have grown even more numerous in the ant's body. They have proliferated around the ant's brain and between surrounding muscle fibers but have not entered the brain, glands, or muscles, making the manipulation all the more amazing.

Ants appear to die within six hours after their final bite. About two to three days later a fungal stalk will start to emerge from the back of the ant's head. After maturing over the course of weeks the stalk's head will shoot spores onto the soil below. Researchers have also discovered that this relatively slow-growing fungus can have its main stem broken off and regrow it later. Foraging worker ants can unwittingly pick up spores as they pass by.

The death of an ant outside of its colony and subsequent growth of the fungal stalk might be key adaptations of the fungus, researchers have hazarded. "Ants quickly remove dead nest mates so that dying in the nest would not allow sufficient time for stalk development and spore release" before the dead host ant was ejected, Hughes and his colleagues noted in their *BMC Ecology* paper.

The doomed ants do not wander too far afield, often ending up within meters of their familiar territory. And large groups of dead ants are commonly found near colonies. These graveyards can contain anywhere from 50 to hundreds of corpses, says Sandra Andersen, currently of the University of Oxford's Department of Zoology, who has studied many of these sites. If a nearby colony is new, there is not likely to be as large a graveyard–yet.

Ants' complex and large social groups are thought to be one of the keys to their global abundance. The fungus has capitalized on ants' social behavior. "Sociality can be thought of as evolution's winning lottery ticket," Hughes says. But "this zombie fungus is natural selection's tax man."

The zombie fungus, however, cannot live without the winning ants' continued success. It appears to be an obligate parasite, requiring a specific, local species of ant for it to inhabit, grow, and propagate its spores.

A Specialized But Global Threat

The ants best known for getting zombified by the *Ophiocordyceps* fungus are tree-dwelling carpenter ants found in Brazil and Thailand, but the fungus is thought to be broadly distributed in tropical areas around the globe. In fact, the full range of strange behavior–observed in Sulawesi, Indonesia–was first described in the scientific literature by Alfred Russell Wallace in the 19th century.

Although many ants in different areas are similarly infected and dispatched in this strange way, the species of fungus infecting them is not at all the same. "Instead of one variable species, there may be tens or even hundreds," says Harry Evans, a principal scientific officer at the Center for Agricultural Bioscience International. In a 2011 paper published in *PLoS ONE*, Evans, Hughes, and Simon Elliot (of the Department of Animal Biology at the Federal University of Vicosa in Brazil) described four new species of the *Ophiocordyceps* fungus that were found in just a small section of rainforest in Brazil's southeastern state of Minas Gerais. Each of these species was associated with a different *Camponotus* ant species, denoting a high degree of specialization.

This hint at such vast diversity and specialization also contains broader implications for assumptions about fungus numbers in general. "We may need to increase fungal diversity estimates by these sorts of factors," Evans notes.

Ancient Scourge

The zombifying fungus's vast geographic distribution also hints at the possibility that it has been possessing ants at least since before many of the continents split apart. But these delicate organisms have not been discovered in fossils. Other examples of parasitism have been found preserved in amber dating back 150 million years, and they reveal the parasite and host as a common arrangement–but not any evidence of actual behavior manipulation.

Research published in *Biology Letters* in 2010 describes a 48-million-year-old fossilized leaf from Germany that bears the distinctive scars of a bite from an ant's mandible on its main vein. The researchers, led by Hughes, describe the find as perhaps "the first example of behavioral manipulation in the fossil record." During that time period the region of Germany would have been similar in climate to the areas of Thailand where contemporary zombie-ant fungus has been documented.

A Parasite's Parasite

The zombie-ant fungus is not the end of the parasitizing line, however–it meets its own death at the work of yet another parasite.

Andersen and her colleagues have found that a different breed of fungi grow over the ant corpse *and* the emerging fungus stalk. By covering the original fungus and its stalk, this secondary fungus–or hyperparasite–effectively prevents the zombie-ant fungus from ejecting its spores. "It looks like they completely sterilize it," Andersen says of the second-level parasite.

Even these hyperparasites seem to be specialized for growing on specific parasitizing fungi. "They're not really growing on anything else" in the area, Andersen says. This makes the hyperparasite another obligate parasite, which depends on the zombie-ant fungus, which depends, in turn, on the carpenter ant colony. "Once you're very successful, something else will take advantage of it," she notes. "It's really a little ecosystem in its own [right]."

The zombie-ant fungus's doom, of course, is little consolation for the infected ant. But the castration of the ant-killing fungus means that it will not go on to turn other local ants into zombies. This hobble might, in fact, be one of the reasons the zombie-ant fungus has been so successful over the long term. As a deadly infection, it could severely damage an ant colony. But, if another parasite renders more than half of its mature spores infertile (and more still failing to reproduce due to other interferences), that creates a sort of equilibrium with a colony. According to the research by Andersen and her colleagues (published in May 2012 in *PLoS ONE*), the actual reproduction rate for each mature zombie-ant fungus organism is a little more than one new mature organism, thus allowing the species and local population to sustain itself as long as there are ants nearby to infect.

In addition to the fungicidal fungi, scientists have also seen small bugs laying their eggs in the infected ant corpse, where their larvae can then eat the growing fungus. These bugs include specialized gall midges (in the Cecidomyiidae family) and a species that appears to be new to science, Hughes says. "It seems their entire nutrition comes from eating the fungus that manipulates ant behavior."

Are such hyper-specialized hyperparasites a freak occurrence? Apparently not: "We have found it all over the world, and most [ant] cadavers have hyperparasites exploiting the zombie-ant fungus at some stage," Hughes notes. And Anderson suspects "the more people study parasites, the more examples we'll find." Even if they are hiding in darker corners.

Indeed, Evans, Hughes, and others continue to hunt for more bizarre, opportunistic organisms. Evans is collecting more zombie-ants in Brazil, as part of what he and Hughes have unofficially dubbed the "World Ant Tour." The hunt may be a race against time, however. When Evans returned to a field site in Ghana where he had found different genera of possessed ants in the 1970s, "we could not find any of the forest sites," he says. They were "all cleared, gone and largely invaded by exotic weeds. In fact, the same thing occurs every time I revisit the places that I have worked over the past 40-plus years," he notes.

Learning about zombie-ant funguses is not simply an exercise in outré science. As Hughes notes, discovering more about both the fungus and the ant behavior and signaling dynamics could add to research about pest control for agriculture. "Lots of the pure discoveries we make have great import for food security and the challenges farmers in tropical countries face from insects and fungi that infect their crops," he notes. But garnering such knowledge will require more zombie corpses to collect and study.

Zombie Insects: A Q&A About a Sinister Virus

By Anna Kuchment

Scientific American contributing editor Anna Kuchment interviews Kelli Hoover, professor of entomology, Pennsylvania State University, University Park, PA.

Q: You recently identified a gene known as egt that allows a specific group of viruses to control the behavior of caterpillars. Tell me what it does.

A: Gypsy moth caterpillars have a normal behavior they do every day. They climb out onto the leaves to feed at night. During the day they climb back onto the branches or bark to hide from predators because they're very obvious when they're on the leaves. But once caterpillars are infected with these viruses, known as baculoviruses, their levels of the EGT protein become elevated. Once that happens, you find them on leaves in the middle of the day. It's like: "What are you doing here?"

Q: And how does that harm the caterpillars?

A: Eventually they climb to the tops of trees, where they get converted into a sac of virus that liquefies and rains virus particles down on the foliage below so that new hosts can be infected by eating the virus on the leaves. Egt is manipulating the insect to die in the right location to transmit the virus to new hosts.

Q: What is the mechanism by which the gene does that?

A: In short, we don't know, but we have a couple of ideas. It was already known that egt blocks molting in caterpillars. What happens when the insects molt is they stop feeding for quite some time; if they're kept from molting, they're kept in a feeding state. It's possible that because they're being stimulated to keep feeding, they're staying up in the tree when everybody else is climbing down.

Q: What are some other viruses that can change host behavior?

A: If you think about rabies, rabies causes the infected animals to come out during the day when they're normally nocturnal, and their behavior becomes more aggressive. There's also a really cool virus that is sexually transmitted in moths. It causes the female moth to keep calling for mates by sending out pheromones, even though she already just mated. That way she infects more and more males. Finally, in toxoplasmosis, cats are the primary host, but mice get infected. When mice are infected, they lose their fear of cats, and they're more likely to get eaten, which allows the pathogen to be transmitted to cats.

Q: What does this mean for humans?

A: It certainly does suggest that other pathogens may contain genes that influence behavior, even in humans. When you have the flu, you cough a lot, which can help transmit the virus to other people. Is that a symptom, or is it the virus making us do that? And has that been selected for through evolution? Who knows?

About the Author

Anna Kuchment is a contributing editor at Scientific American *and a staff science reporter at the* Dallas Morning News*. She is also co-author of a forthcoming book about earthquakes triggered by energy production.*

Attack of the Zombie Maker

By Kenneth C. Catania

The emerald jewel wasp is a cockroach's worst nightmare

"You still don't understand what you're dealing with, do you? Perfect organism. Its structural perfection is matched only by its hostility.... I admire its purity. A survivor, unclouded by conscience, remorse or delusions of morality." That is how the android Ash famously describes filmmaker Ridley Scott's extraterrestrial monster in the 1979 blockbuster *Alien*. The movie provided nightmare fodder for an entire generation of science-fiction fans with its tale of an alien creature that attaches itself to the face of a crew member of the spaceship *Nostromo* and implants an embryo that later bursts from his chest. Technically speaking, the alien is a parasitoid, an organism that, unlike most parasites, ultimately kills its host. No one who has seen the film will ever forget how it reproduces, even if they want to.

Recently I have come to share some of Ash's sentiments about chest-bursting parasitoids. But don't judge me too harshly. I am not talking about monster parasitoids from outer space. I am referring to what seems to be the closest thing we have here on Earth: the parasitoid emerald jewel wasp, *Ampulex compressa*, which makes zombies (and worse) out of the American cockroach.

To give you a little background, I am a neurobiologist, and every fall I teach a course about animal brains and behavior at Vanderbilt University. On Halloween I like to showcase an appropriately creepy bit of biology as a memorable way for students to learn some basic neuroscience. When I began teaching about the emerald jewel wasp, I became so intrigued by the species that I just had to bring some of the wasps to my laboratory to see their behavior for myself. I started with a simple plan to take pictures and make some videos for my class, but soon I found myself carrying out research on this striking insect. The jewel wasp was already well known for being a parasitoid, but through my experiments over the past few years,

I have learned that it is even more remarkable than researchers previously understood. And the roach, it turns out, has a nifty trick of its own.

Taking Control

Before I tell you what I discovered that filled me with admiration for this creature, I should explain how it first gained notoriety. Every female jewel wasp is on a mission. To reproduce, the wasp needs to find a host that will supply the necessary food for her young. Like many parasitoid species, the emerald jewel wasp is a specialist with only one option for a host–in this case, the American cockroach, *Periplaneta americana*. This target is one reason the jewel wasp is so popular even among insectophobes: as the proverb goes, the enemy of your enemy is your friend.

Among biologists, however, the emerald jewel wasp elicits respect for its remarkable attack strategy. Frederic Libersat of Ben-Gurion University of the Negev in Israel and his colleagues–including venom specialist Michael Adams of the University of California, Riverside–have conducted a series of elegant studies that tell a story rivaling science fiction. It all starts when a female wasp locates an unfortunate cockroach.

The jewel wasp has an incredibly nuanced attack. It takes a neurosurgical approach to paralyzing its host, first stinging the cockroach directly in a part of the central nervous system called the first thoracic ganglion. This structure houses the motor neurons that control the roach's front legs. The wasp's venom contains gamma-aminobutyric acid (GABA), an inhibitory neurotransmitter that shuts down the motor neurons, temporarily paralyzing the legs. This first surgical strike leaves the roach unable to protect its head from the next sting, which the wasp directs through the soft membranes of the roach's throat and straight into its brain. This second dose of venom has the insidious effect of changing the roach from a violently struggling (and dangerous) opponent into a compliant and pacified host–that is, a zombie.

From there things go predictably downhill for the roach. The venom injected during the brain sting includes the neurotransmitter dopamine, which causes the roach to incessantly groom its legs and antennae when it should instead be trying to escape. In the meantime, the wasp goes in search of a crypt in which it can entomb the roach with an egg. Once it finds a suitable location, the wasp returns to the roach and does something that might seem gratuitous in a horror movie. It grasps one of the roach's sensitive antennae and bites off most of its length, leaving only a bleeding stump. It then does the same to the other antenna, and it uses the stumps like straws to drink the cockroach's blood. You can think of roach blood as the wasp's favorite supplement, providing energy and nutrients after the intense struggle (I do not see the fad catching on). Next, the wasp grasps one of the antenna stumps and, walking backward, pulls the cockroach forward. The cockroach follows like a dog on a leash. Once they are inside the tomb, the wasp glues a single small egg on one of the roach's two middle legs. Then it exits the tomb and uses nearby debris to securely block the entrance before departing.

Take a moment to consider this astounding product of evolution. For any predator, it is plenty hard to stalk, catch, and kill elusive prey. The emerald jewel wasp has an even greater challenge–taking its prey prisoner so it can serve as a living larder for the larva when it eventually hatches. To do so, the jewel wasp must deliver venom to two small neural targets inside the armored body of an insect that specializes in escaping from threats. No other animal that scientists know of has such a sophisticated means of manipulating another animal's nervous system. And yet there is more to the story.

A Mother's Touch

It is safe to say that no one ever walked away from watching *Alien* wondering about the trials and tribulations of the poor little chest-bursting parasitoid that scurried off the lunch table in the *Nostromo*. Much the same could be said for the typical view of the jewel wasp's larva. Even scientists studying the wasp usually cut to the credits once the wasp seals the cockroach in the tomb. It is assumed that the larva will hatch from the tiny egg, find a soft spot from which to feed, and break through the cuticle to eat the living cockroach from the inside, later emerging from the roach triumphant in a familiar, *Alien*-parasitoid fashion.

But life is not so easy for a hopeful chest burster, as I had occasion to learn when I was distracted by other projects and my wasp colony almost died out. It was only then that I tracked each larva, hoping I would end up with enough wasps to resurrect the colony. The colony survived, but from this experience I learned that the tiny, soft-bodied wasp larva is not very competent. Unlike the frighteningly dexterous face huggers in *Alien*, a wasp grub moves slowly, if at all, and it can feed successfully only at one soft membrane on the cockroach. If it misses the target by a fraction of a millimeter, it dies (and the lucky roach recovers from the brain sting after about a week).

The grub's fragility puts a lot of pressure on the mother wasp, who must glue its egg in just the right location for its young to survive. How does the wasp do it? To explore this question, I flipped a microscope upside down and bolted it to a table, and then I arranged a clear-bottomed chamber as a tomb for the wasp to find. This rig allowed me to get a close-up recording of the entire egg-laying process. The video showed the wasp making a very thorough investigation of the cockroach leg with the tip of its abdomen before laying the egg right next to a weak spot in the roach's armor. (Like all insects, cockroaches have a tough exoskeleton, but just like medieval armor, the exoskeleton has weak points at the joints.) When I looked at the tip of the wasp's abdomen under a scanning electron microscope, I noticed an array of minuscule hairs, almost like a set of miniature whiskers. Could these be the sensors the wasp uses to find the right location for the egg?

To test this possibility, I anesthetized wasps and trimmed off the hairs. That might sound simple enough to do, but it is a comically delicate operation that I could carry out only by holding the groggy (soon to be very angry) wasp with two bare fingers while gently shaving the equivalent of its private parts with an ultrasharp obsidian scalpel. It is a good setup for the ultimate fail. But it worked, and the results confirmed my suspicion: hairless wasps had trouble finding the right spot to place the egg. This observation not only revealed a key sensor used in the egg-laying process but also confirmed the critical importance of proper egg placement—a larva that hatched in the wrong place usually died without finding the roach's weak spot.

Chance Discovery

While I was studying the wasp's sensory hairs and larval survival, I discovered something else that was entirely unexpected. Before each female wasp found the sweet spot for its egg, it extended the tip of its abdomen and repeatedly probed the center of the cockroach in front of the middle legs. In response, the cockroach often extended the middle leg on the side where the wasp was, as if annoyed by having its underside poked.

At first I did not know what to make of this behavior. It seemed like a distraction from the wasp's egg-laying mission, as well as from my own mission of trying to understand the role of the wasp's sensory hairs. But eventually I decided to look more closely at the wasp's probing behavior by increasing the magnification of my microscope. I was astounded to see that the wasp was not just feeling around under the roach. Rather I could see the wasp's stinger as it extended below the roach's partially transparent cuticle. How could this be? Everyone who studies the jewel wasp knows it stings the roach twice—once in the first thoracic ganglion to paralyze the front legs and once in the brain to zombify the roach. Perhaps I was seeing a confused wasp, an outlier that was behaving abnormally.

I decided to change my focus, both literally and figuratively, and follow up on this observation. I soon learned that before laying an egg, every female jewel wasp delivers three stings to the central portion of the roach's body under a very specific part of its armor called the basisternum. This structure is situated directly over the second thoracic ganglion, another part of the cockroach's central nervous system. Recall that the wasp's first sting goes into the first thoracic ganglion, paralyzing the front legs during the initial attack. The second thoracic ganglion, as you might guess, houses the motor neurons that control the second pair of legs, one of which the wasp will choose as the site for its egg. I realized that the odd leg-extension behavior I had noticed occurred within a few seconds of the newly documented stings. It seemed that the wasp's sting was somehow forcing the roach to move its leg. Could this be one more stage in the wasp's process of establishing mind control over the cockroach?

It seemed possible, but how could I ever tell whether the sting was actually directed into the second thoracic ganglion, which is inside the roach's body? The same question had been asked about the wasp's first sting into the first thoracic ganglion, and it was a matter of long-standing debate until Libersat finally solved the mystery once and for all with an ingenious approach. He made the wasp, and thus its venom, radioactive. After the wasp stung the cockroach, he was able to show that the first thoracic ganglion contained the radioactivity.

I confess that I am not so brave as Libersat when it comes to making wasps radioactive—or to undertaking all the paperwork involved in getting the necessary permission to do such a thing. Fortunately, there was a more direct way to find out where the wasp was stinging. I anesthetized a cockroach and cut a small window into its cuticle so that the ganglion was visible. Then I increased my microscope's magnification and watched as the wasp stung. Sure enough, the sting was directed into the ganglion. (This approach would not work for tracing the first sting, which occurs during a pitched battle with the wasp.) Better yet, the sting was aimed at the side of the ganglion controlling the leg on the same side as the wasp—the side where it would later glue its egg. It is pretty clear that the wasp's venom during these later stings contains a component that activates the motor neurons in the second thoracic ganglion, thus causing the leg to extend.

But why would such a remarkably specialized behavior evolve? In other words, how does extending the roach's leg help the wasp reproduce? This time the answer was obvious. When the cockroach folds up its middle leg, the wasp cannot explore the surface with its sensory hairs to find the sweet spot for its egg where the larva can later feed and break into the cockroach. By hijacking the neural circuit that causes leg extension, the wasp removes the last barrier the roach might use to defend itself from a ghastly fate. How the venom causes this response is unknown, but we do know which neurotransmitter probably activates the target neurons: acetylcholine. Many wasps have acetylcholine in their venom, and it would likely be sufficient to activate the motor neurons and cause the observed leg extension. More study is needed to determine whether this simple explanation is correct, however, or whether some other venom component is involved.

Perhaps you can now see why I am so impressed with the jewel wasp. It has evolved the behavior and the venom needed to sequentially target three small spots in the roach's nervous system. Each sting has a different effect, and each allows the wasp to bend its victim to its will, ultimately leaving the usually elusive and dangerous cockroach alive and at the mercy of a delicate little grub. It all seems pretty hopeless for the roach, much as it did for the crew of the *Nostromo* in Alien. But the Alien met its match in Ellen Ripley, famously played by Sigourney Weaver. What happens when a wasp meets the Ripley of the cockroach world?

Making a Stand

So far I have told you how a wasp defeats a cockroach with multiple stings to its central nervous system. The outcome seems inevitable if the roach is surprised by the wasp or if it runs. In those cases, the wasp easily gets the upper hand either by grabbing the roach immediately or by chasing it down–a roach cannot outrun a flying wasp. Once the wasp's jaws have closed on the cockroach, it can usually deliver the first sting within about a second, paralyzing the front legs, and—well, you know the grim story from there.

But some roaches have an attitude. They are vigilant, watching and feeling with their long antennae for an approaching threat. When a wasp closes in, these roaches do not run. Instead they get ready for a fight, raising themselves to full height by extending their long, spiny legs. In this so-called stilt-standing posture, the roach appears very much like a fencer in the en garde position, and in fact the stance seems to serve a similar purpose: it raises the roach's body away from the wasp, making it a more distant and difficult target. At the same time, the roach's legs present a phalanx of sharp spines to the wasp as it tries to reach the roach's vulnerable body. The wasp cannot deliver the first sting until it has grabbed hold of the roach. The two contestants circle each other, advancing and retreating in turn. Often the wasp will make a lunge at the cockroach, which bobs and weaves to avoid the clamping jaws before reestablishing its defensive stance.

But the real surprise for me (and seemingly for the wasp) during my observations of such encounters came in the form of powerful kicks delivered by the cockroach with its spiny hind legs. These kicks often landed squarely on the wasp's head and shoved the wasp through the air until it crashed into the nearest object. The wasp inevitably dusted itself off with a quick bout of grooming and resumed the attack, at least after the first kick. But if the cockroach managed to land multiple kicks, the wasp usually broke off its attack. Apparently, to avoid becoming zombies and then having an alien burst from their bodies, roaches have to use the same strategy as many a science-fiction character: stay vigilant, don't run, and aim for the attacker's head.

About the Author

Kenneth C. Catania is a professor of biological sciences at Vanderbilt University. He studies comparative neurobiology with an emphasis on animal sensory systems. His latest book is Great Adaptations *(Princeton University Press, 2020).*

GLOSSARY

anthropomorphize To attribute human characteristics to nonhuman things and creatures.

asymptomatic Showing no symptoms.

automaton A mechanical device that is made to look like a human.

bipedalism A form of locomotion by an organism achieved by using two rear limbs or legs.

bokor A witch or priest in the Vodoun religion who uses both light and dark magic.

bystander effect A theory in social psychology that claims people are less willing to help others when there are other people around.

chauvinism Belief in the superiority of one's own group, sex, or place.

corporeal Having to do with the material body; not spiritual.

cryptozoology The study of legendary animals to determine whether or not they exist.

epidemiological Having to do with causes, distribution, and control of health-related states, such as diseases, in a population.

episodic Temporary or occurring at irregular intervals.

Galileo Effect A belief that persists despite a lack of evidence for it or despite compelling evidence against it.

hallucination An experience of perceiving something that isn't real or present.

hedonist A person for whom pleasure is the most important part of life.

hirsutism A condition in which women grow dark, coarse hair in places more common for men.

immortal Never dying; living forever.

mediumship The practice of producing mental or physical phenomena by communicating with the deceased or other spiritual beings.

metaphysical Describing an idea or reality that is outside of what human beings perceive.

monotonic Neither increasing nor decreasing as the independent variable increases.

neuropharmacological Having to do with the ways drugs affect the nervous system and influence behavior.

neuroscience The scientific study of the nervous system.

paranormal psychology The scientific study of the human mind in relation to psychic phenomena and other paranormal claims.

parapsychologist A person who studies paranormal psychology.

parasite An organism that lives on or in another organism and benefits at the other organism's expense.

scintilla A tiny amount of something.

social psychology The study of how the behaviors, feelings, and thoughts of people are affected by the presence of others in a society.

ubiquity The state of being everywhere or in many places at once.

Vodoun A religion derived from Africa and practiced primarily in Haiti that involves polytheism (belief in many gods) and ancestor worship; also called "voodoo."

xenophobia Fear of anything foreign or strange, particularly other groups of people.

FURTHER INFORMATION

Blumenthal, Ralph, and Leslie Kean. "Navy Reports Describe Encounters with Unexplained Flying Objects." *New York Times*, May 14, 2020 (updates July 24, 2020), www.nytimes.com/2020/05/14/us/politics/navy-ufo-reports.html.

Crair, Ben. "Why Do So Many People Still Want to Believe in Bigfoot?" *Smithsonian Magazine*, September 2018, www.smithsonianmag.com/history/why-so-many-people-still-believe-in-bigfoot-180970045/.

Hefferon, Michael. "The Medical Science Behind Ancient Vampire Myths." Healthcare-in-Europe.com, May 7, 2020, https://healthcare-in-europe.com/en/news/the-medical-science-behind-ancient-vampire-myths.html.

Kambhampaty, Anna P. "Many Americans Say They Believe in Ghosts. Do You?" *New York Times*, October 28, 2021, www.nytimes.com/2021/10/28/style/do-you-believe-in-ghosts.html.

Karasz, Palko. "Now There's an Event to Storm Loch Ness and 'Find Dat Big Boi.'" *New York Times*, July 24, 2019, www.nytimes.com/2019/07/24/world/europe/loch-ness-monster-area-51.html.

Radford, Benjamin, and Patrick Pester. "Bigfoot: Is the Sasquatch Real?" LiveScience.com, January 14, 2022, www.livescience.com/24598-bigfoot.html.

Stierwalt, Sabrina, Ph.D. "Real-Life Zombies." Quick and Dirty Tips, May 13, 2019, www.quickanddirtytips.com/education/science/real-life-zombies?utm_source=sciam&utm_campaign=sciam.

Wilson, Edward O. "The Zombie Ants." *New York Times*, August 21, 2020, www.nytimes.com/2020/08/21/opinion/sunday/zombie-ants.html.

Zinoman, Jason. "Why the Vampire Myth Won't Die." *New York Times*, October 30, 2021, www.nytimes.com/2021/10/30/style/vampires-coronavirus.html.

CITATIONS

1.1 The Zombies in Our Midst by Melanie Tannenbaum (October 31, 2013); 1.2 Born to the Purple: The Story of Porphyria by Nick Lane (December 16, 2002); 1.3 Mummy DNA Reveals Birth of Ancient Scourge by David Biello (October 6, 2006); 1.4 In a First, Physicists Glimpse a Quantum Ghost by Karmela Padavic-Callaghan (December 8, 2021); 1.5 Scientific American vs. the Supernatural by Katherine Harmon Courage (September 1, 2020); 1.6 Should Scientists Take UFOs and Ghosts More Seriously? by John Horgan (May 18, 2020); 1.7 If Bigfoot Were Real by Darren Naish (June 27, 2016); 2.1 Ghost Lusters: If You Want to See a Specter Badly Enough, Will You? by Adam Marcus (October 27, 2008); 2.2 Ghost Stories: Visits from the Deceased by Vaughan Bell (December 2, 2008); 2.3 How Chasing Bigfoot Can Lead to Actual Science by Alison Gilchrist (May 3, 2018); 2.4 Here Be Dragons by Kelly Reidy (May 10, 2019); 2.5 The American Fascination with Zombies by Krystal D'Costa (October 26, 2011); 2.6 Why We Are So Intrigued by Zombies by Michael Shermer (January 1, 2015); 2.7 Zombie Fever: A Mathematician Studies a Pop Culture Epidemic by Evelyn Lamb (October 30, 2013); 3.1 How Would Immortality Affect a Vampire's Memory? by Brian Levine (August 20, 2014); 3.2 Bigfoot Anatomy by Marguerite Holloway (December 1, 2007); 3.3 A True and Complete Account of the Neuroscience of Zombies by Gareth Cook (November 18, 2014); 3.4 Can You Escape Zombies If You Smell Like Death? by Josh Fischman (October 30, 2014); 3.5 Avoiding Zombie Attacks with Social Psychology by Melanie Tannenbaum (October 31, 2015); 3.6 Bugs in the Brain by Robert Sapolsky (March 1, 2003); 3.7 Protozoa Could Be Controlling Your Brain by Christof Koch (May 1, 2011); 3.8 Played by a Parasite by Gustavo Arrizabalaga and Bill Sullivan (March 1, 2015); 3.9 Microbes on Your Mind by Moheb Costandi (July 1, 2012); 3.10 You Know Those Parasites That Control Our Brains? by Bradley von Paridon (November 18, 2014); 4.1 Blood Ties: Vampire Bats Build Trust to Become Food-Sharing Pals by Jason G. Goldman (March 19, 2020); 4.2 Pharaohs Got Yummy Mummy Meals by Cynthia Graber (November 26, 2011); 4.3 Your Average, Everyday Zombie by Christie Wilcox (October 31, 2011); 4.4 Zombie Creatures: What Happens When Animals Are Possessed by a Parasitic Puppet Master? by Katherine Harmon (October 30, 2009); 4.5 How This Zombie Fungus Turns Cicadas into Horror-Movie Sex Bots by Rachel Nuwer (May 27, 2021); 4.6 Zombie Cicadas' Bodies Are Literally Falling Apart by Jennifer Frazer (April 16, 2018); 4.7 Undead-End: Fungus That Controls Zombie-Ants Has Own Fungal Stalker by Katherine Harmon (November 8, 2012); 4.8 Zombie Insects: A Q&A About a Sinister Virus by Anna Kuchment (November 1, 2011); 4.9 Attack of the Zombie Maker by Kenneth C. Catania (February 1, 2021).

Each author biography was accurate at the time the article was originally published.

INDEX